IN HER BED

The Desperadoes 2

Jan Springer

MENAGE AMOUR

Siren Publishing, Inc.
www.SirenPublishing.com

A SIREN PUBLISHING BOOK
IMPRINT: Ménage Amour

IN HER BED
Copyright © 2011 by Jan Springer

ISBN-10: 1-61926-064-6
ISBN-13: 978-1-61926-064-1

First Printing: October 2011

Cover design by Jinger Heaston
All cover art and logo copyright © 2011 by Siren Publishing, Inc.

Printed in the U.S.A.

PUBLISHER
Siren Publishing, Inc.
www.SirenPublishing.com

IN HER BED

The Desperadoes 2

JAN SPRINGER
Copyright © 2011

Chapter One

Dr. Elizabeth Brandywine sensed the men in her bedroom even before she opened her eyes. There were three of them, all gorgeously naked, their tanned bodies laced with corded muscles. She'd always loved a man with muscles, and these guys were loaded with them. Even their muscles had muscles. Oh sweet mercy, it was suddenly getting quite hot beneath her comforters.

Mixed emotions swept through her as her gaze drifted to the man standing in the middle of the trio. His gaze locked onto hers. She could read the hunger tensing his body. The intent flaring in his eyes.

Durango. He'd come back. He'd brought Landon and a third man. She knew why they were here.

A strangled sob tore at her throat. Would Durango push her past her boundaries this time?

In the early morning sunshine, their eyes glistened with unmistakable lust, and their huge cocks were fully erect as they stroked themselves and looked at her. Elizabeth swallowed against her nervousness and tried to calm her pulse.

Ethan Durango had returned, and she knew she'd regret it if she told him to go away again.

"Landon and I have been wanting you, Doc," Durango whispered.

Landon. The man Durango had wanted her to sleep with before they'd both left. The man she'd wanted to have sex with, but didn't dare because she hadn't been ready to dive into that lifestyle.

"Are you naked for us beneath those covers, Doc?" Durango asked as he reached down and began tugging the comforters off her body. "I told you when I came back I wanted you naked for us, baby."

Liz creamed at his words. Muscles in his arms bulged and her breath halted in her lungs as he began to pull on the comforter. Her heart began to thump madly as the cover dipped over her heaving breasts. The other two men tensed. Waited. Watched. Their heated gazes studied the comforter as it lowered.

Cool night air breathed against her breasts as she was revealed to them. The men sucked in their breaths with appreciation. Excitement burst through her, and she trembled. The covers continued to lower, and cool air breathed against her belly and then her pussy.

Oh God. She was completely bared to them.

His wild male scent swept around her as Durango climbed up on the foot of the bed, his calloused palms sliding up the insides of her ankles. His hands were like heat lightning shimmering over her flesh, and she automatically widened her legs for him. Her breath halted as she watched the other two men. They didn't move. They stayed in their places, transfixed by what Durango was doing. They were watching. Waiting for their turn.

Oh God.

She moaned as Durango's large shoulders pushed her thighs further apart as he moved into position between her legs. His bunched muscles ignited sensations along the insides of her legs wherever he touched, and he was touching everywhere.

"You know what we want, Doc. You know we want you," he breathed.

She twisted against him, loving the erotic way his hot breath caressed her pussy. She tensed as the other two men suddenly came up either side of the bed. Her fists grabbed the sheets, knotting in them.

She shouldn't let this happen. She shouldn't. But she wanted to break through her walls and just cut loose. To finally find her sexual self and be free.

The two men were climbing onto the bed now, their big, strong bodies rippling with hard muscles. Her mouth went dry with increased nervousness as they lay beside her. She gasped and whimpered as each of them cupped one breast.

"Do you want us, Liz?" Durango's deep voice caused all her nerve endings to stand at attention. She looked down over her tight belly to where his head was poised. Eagerness and readiness shone brightly in his eyes.

She wished she could say yes, she was ready. Wanted to say yes, but the words wouldn't come out of her mouth.

The two men at her breasts continued massaging her mounds, squeezing her nipples until she ached for them to take her into their mouths. She arched against Durango as he lowered his head to between her thighs again. His tongue parted her labia and slid over her engorged, pulsing clit. He swept over her ultrasensitive flesh in slow erotic circles that had her pussy creaming and her body tightening with need.

His hands skimmed up and down the length of her hips, pumping her arousal. His lips sucked on her labia, making her thrust her hips against him. The sensations his succulent mouth created rocked her to her very core.

"All you have to do is say yes, Doc," Durango said as he moved his mouth away from her hot pussy. He stared up at her, his face twisted in anticipation, his eyelids lowered to half-mast, partially hiding his lust-flared blue eyes.

"Please," she whispered.

Her cunt clenched with a fierce need to be filled.

"Please, take me."

Durango grinned with satisfaction, and her heart bounced with happiness. His large hands came off her hips and around to splay over her sensitized abdomen. She cried out as his head disappeared between her thighs again. Fingers spread her labia, and she fought for control as his mouth fused over her entire pussy.

The two men at each of her breasts were lowering their heads, and Liz cried out her satisfaction as two mouths melted over her nipples. Pressure and arousal mingled as they pressed their faces into her breasts. Their teeth held her nipples captive as they lashed their tongues against her there.

Sweet mercy, such perfection.

Her thighs tightened around Durango's shoulders. Lifting her knees, she brought her feet up and over his backside, digging her heels into his rock-hard ass. She moaned as the bristles on his chin and cheeks rubbing her inner thighs sparked more arousal. She felt the same erotic abrasion from the two men sucking on her nipples.

She wrenched her hips as a finger slipped into her drenched channel. He brought his finger out and kept sucking her pussy. How he could do both, she'd no idea, but she loved the dual sensations of mouth sucking and a finger slipping in and out of her. The pressure on her breasts increased as the men cupped her harder, their mouths pushing into her pillows, their teeth clenching her nipples until the sweetest pleasure-pain shattered her senses.

She growled encouragement and ground her hips harder against Durango's head, straining her upper body against their erotic mouths, bringing herself closer to orgasm. Her body grew hot and taut. She tensed and readied herself to come. Oh yes, she could feel it building now. She was going to come...

An odd squeak shot Dr. Elizabeth Brandywine right out of her erotic-drenched dream, forcing her to open her eyes. For the briefest second she embraced the flare of arousal tensing her body, loved the way a hand was clenched against her pussy, the other hand pressing on her left breast. She felt hot. So freaking hot and so sexually aware, she almost began masturbating.

Then reality crashed around her, and her arousal vanished. Something was wrong. The room was dark, too dark. She blinked wildly, trying to orient herself, and immediately heard the patter of rain, but nothing else.

Had she imagined that squeak? Had it been a sound in her dream? It may even have been a branch scratching against a window. Or maybe it had just been the couch springs squeaking as she'd shifted in her sleep?

Restlessness made her breathing unsteady, and she felt a chill in the air. That meant the fire in the hearth had died and it should be close to dawn now. In her occupation as a doctor, she was used to unexpected visitors at all times of the day and night, but people always knocked. Had she been so soundly asleep that someone had knocked and she hadn't heard?

A soft rumble of thunder drifted through the room, and the creepy sound made her burrow deeper beneath the feather comforter. She shivered with unease. Thunder. That was what it must have been.

Yeah, right.

She forced herself to steady her breathing. Forced herself to stay calm. What if someone had opened the front door? Maybe that was the squeak she'd heard? Maybe an intruder had heard it, too, and decided to find another way into her home?

Elizabeth swallowed and listened. The rain continued to patter, and her eyes widened with icy shivers of horror that slashed through her as a shadow passed the window.

Oh damn! It was nights like these she wished she didn't live alone so far from town or from her nearest neighbor. Someone was out there, and they weren't knocking. That meant only one thing. Bad news for her.

Cold adrenaline rocked her, and she grabbed the gun she kept nestled on top of the nearby coffee table. In a flash, she scurried off the couch and shivered as the icy night air blasted against her thin nightgown.

Quickly, she went to the window where she'd seen the shadow pass. Moving the lace curtain slightly aside, she peered out. The green glow of the aurora borealis shimmered in the night sky, illuminating her yard, but nothing moved.

Suddenly Elizabeth wished for the old days. Days before the Catastrophe when a quick call to 911 would deliver the help she needed. But the Catastrophe had screwed everything. Solar flares had disintegrated most of her family and friends and fried all the electrical grids worldwide. There were no phone connections around these parts. No 911. No help. She was totally on her own. She should have been used to this new way of life by now. She wasn't.

Trembling, she clutched the gun tighter in the palm of her hand and made her way into the adjoining kitchen and into the hall foyer. She froze as another volley of icy shivers paralyzed her. The front door stood wide open.

Oh my God!

Someone was in her house. She needed to run as fast as she could. Knowing it would be very cold outside and she would have trouble scrambling over the rocky terrain in her bare feet, she thought about grabbing her shoes and coat, but she couldn't remember where she'd put them. No use looking. She'd waste precious time. She'd take her chances outdoors.

She had to get out. Now. She almost did that. Almost bolted out the open doorway, but someone suddenly appeared there.

Panic took hold. Forgetting the gun in her hand, she turned and ran back down the hallway, through the kitchen, and past the living room. She'd dive out the window. That was what she'd do. No, she couldn't do that. She'd cut herself with the broken glass. She'd have to go out the back door.

Her heart smashed against her chest as the man shouted at her from behind. Something about him not going to hurt her.

Yeah, right. She wasn't in the mood to be kept alive while someone sawed off her arms and legs, one at a time, and made shish kebabs of her body parts and ate them right in front of her. She'd heard stories of that happening. People were scared and hungry since the Catastrophe, and they were literally eating each other in order to survive. She'd even cauterized a woman's arm after the woman had escaped the thugs who'd been keeping her just so they could eat her.

Or worse, since she was a doctor, he might be here to kidnap her and force her to keep his victims alive. Maybe even force her to do the amputations and then treat them in order to keep their food sources alive for as long as possible.

Oh my God, she was being morbid. She needed to ditch these hideous thoughts before she started screaming. Rushing to the back door, she fumbled with the lock. That's when she remembered the gun in her hand.

Sweet mercy! Was she an idiot or what? In her panic, she'd forgotten the gun. *Shoot him. Turn around and shoot.*

She ignored that idea, preferring to escape. Maybe she could get out and no one would get hurt. She could run to her closest neighbor, Teyla Sutton. Teyla had three men living with her. They would help her.

Allowing a panicked sob to escape, she opened the door and screamed with shock as a tall man stood there, his face hidden in darkness. She was trapped!

She screamed again as someone grabbed her from behind. An arm snapped around her waist like a steel band. Her finger tightened on the trigger, and the gun went off. Her captor wrenched the gun away from her.

Stupid woman. You should have killed the bastards the moment you saw them.

Panic slashed through her like a meat cleaver, making her breathless as her feet left the floor. He carried her back down the hallway. She kept screaming. She couldn't help it.

They were going to kill her. Or rape her. Or worse!

She realized the other man, the one in the back doorway, had disappeared. Maybe she'd hit him when the gun had gone off? Maybe she could still escape?

She began kicking at the guy holding her captive. She hit somewhere solid. His grip loosened. She used her elbows and found more solid flesh. A couple of loud *oomphs* encouraged her to keep fighting. Without warning, he let go of her, and she was sailing through the air. She fell onto the couch, the one she'd been sleeping on. The sagging springs creaked as she hit them hard. Then, he flew on top of her, his big body crushing her beneath his heavy weight, pinning her. She tried to scream, realized she still was screaming.

A cold hand clamped over her mouth, and for some unexplainable reason she stopped screaming. An eerie silence followed, and she stopped struggling, realizing screaming was wasting precious energy.

Her captor was breathing hard. They were both breathing hard. She tensed as a familiar voice, one etched with humor, whispered into her ear. "Hey, Brandy, we've missed you."

Relief, lightning quick, sliced through her.

It was Landon Leigh.

Liz swallowed as a hot flush of warmth splashed through her. Brandy. That was Landon's nickname for her.

Suddenly she became aware of his every hard, heated muscle as he pressed against her flesh. Noticed the powerful grip of his thighs wrapped around her legs. The strong arms that held her wrists prevented her from hitting him as anger slashed through her. The bastard had nerve, scaring her the way he had. She was about to cut into him with a volley of curses when his next words stopped her cold.

"We need your services," he said.

Her services? Elizabeth blinked in stunned disbelief and tried to still her racing thoughts. Hell, who was she kidding? She couldn't even form a thought. All she knew was she needed to get away from Landon, because she suspected she knew who the other man standing at the back door would be. She knew why they'd come here.

A slow, erotic tremble began to shift through her body. Oh yes, she needed to escape.

"There's three wounded," Landon whispered.

He lifted his hand from her mouth, and her first instinct was to start screaming again because she was that pumped with adrenaline. He moved off her, and she could see a silhouette of another man standing nearby.

"Long time, no see, Doc," that man said in a steely voice that, despite it sounding icy and angry, smoothed over her trembling body like hot liquid fire.

It was Ethan Durango. Her ex-fiancé. Son of a bitch! She should have recognized him. Should have recognized both of them. But she'd been too scared. Or maybe deep down she'd known all along who they were and why they'd come?

She bolted from the couch before she even realized she was doing it. How dare they scare her so badly? How bloody well dare they!

Fully intending to slap Durango silly, she raised her arm, but he was faster. Durango was always faster. He grabbed her wrist, his fingers digging into her flesh like steel bands.

"Uh-uh. No slapping, Doc. I'm the only one allowed to do that, remember?" His sultry voice sent tremors coursing through her. She knew what he meant. He enjoyed slapping her ass. Spanking her until she blushed before he took her.

Well, not this time around. She'd kicked him out months ago after he'd revealed he and his friend, Landon, had sexual fantasies of what they wanted to do to her. She'd been so embarrassed and shy because she'd wanted the same thing that she'd been unable to confess to that truth to Durango.

"Get out of here. Both of you," she said as the familiar anger and shame raged through her.

"You'd turn away three patients, Doc? You'd put our lives in danger because you can't face the truth?"

Doc. His nickname for her. When they'd been engaged she'd loved it when he called her that. Now it just pissed her off because it reminded her of the wonderful carefree days they'd shared before the Catastrophe. It had been another life. He'd been another man back then. The Catastrophe had changed all that. Changed both of them.

"It's your truth. Not mine. Now get out," she spat.

Although it was dark in the living room, she could see the irritation flare in his eyes. Could feel his body tense with fury.

She tried to get away from him, to break his grip. Of course, he wouldn't allow that.

"She's a hellfire, that's for sure." The words were soft-spoken with underlying lust and appreciation from Landon. Although she'd only known Landon a few short months while he'd worked here, she knew she should have recognized him standing in front of her. Should have realized he would never hurt her. Hell, he was the man who wanted to fuck her while Durango watched. Suddenly her cheeks warmed. It irritated her.

"If you wanted my help, you should have knocked. Now get out, and don't come back."

"Maybe you shouldn't have been so deep in your dreams, baby," Durango said.

Her cheeks grew hot at his knowing comment.

"Besides, you shot me, Doc. The least you can do is fix me up before you send us on our way."

Liz blinked as a shock wave rolled over her. She'd shot him? *Oh my God.* She'd shot Durango when the gun went off? Concern washed away her anger.

"Where are you hit?"

Before he could answer, she saw the dark stain on the upper right arm area of his jacket.

Okay, calm down. He was still standing, so it wasn't that bad. But she also knew how quickly a gunshot wound could get infected.

"Take off your shirt. I'll get my bag."

She tried to get out of Durango's grasp again, but he didn't let loose. Instead, he nodded to Landon.

"You'll take care of the others first. Landon, you get her bag. She usually keeps it in the hall closet by the front door. Top shelf."

Landon nodded, and he hurried away. That was when she realized Landon was limping. Another wave of concern snapped through her. She'd need to tend to Landon, too. Durango had mentioned three wounded. Where was the third man? And was that what her hot dream had been about? A forewarning of things to come?

Liz shook her head in denial. Tried to ignore the intense awareness of Durango and Landon washing through her, but she knew the longer they stayed in her home, the harder it would be to keep them away from her.

She knew they'd joined the Durango Gang. It was a Robin Hood-type gang his oldest surviving cousin, Kayne Durango, had started. Unfortunately in their quest to steal from the rich and give to the poor, every vigilante group that made money off the misery of others wanted the Durango Gang to hang by the neck until they were dead. She'd told Durango if he joined his cousin's gang and became a desperado, he wasn't welcome back here. The minute he'd left, she realized she'd never really meant it. She still loved him, no matter how much he'd changed. *Or how much he'd tried to get you to confront your own sexual demons.*

"We didn't see your horse in the lean-to out back. Thought maybe you weren't living here anymore," Durango said, his grip on her wrist tightening. "I should have known you'd be deep in your fantasies, baby. When you're dreaming, an earthquake can't wake you. Much to my annoyance, of course, when I want to make love to you."

Intense heat flared through her, and she forced herself to ignore his latter comment.

"I loaned the horse to a neighbor." She'd lent the horse to Teyla and her men for a few days.

She could feel the heat from Durango's body now. Could smell his scent. Rich and dangerous, yet soothing at the same time. Durango, as she'd always called him, had always kept her off-balance. She loved that about him. At least she had loved him, until his confession that he wanted to make both their sexual fantasies come true. She forced herself to shake away those thoughts. *Time to deal with reality.*

"You said there are three wounded. Where's the other one?"

Heavy footsteps from the front of the house made her look toward the doorway where Landon had exited a moment earlier. This time, he'd returned with a man, who leaned against him.

"That would be him, Tyrell Mathews. He's been shot in the waist." Durango replied.

"When did this happen?" She would need to know if infection had already set in.

"Just yesterday," Durango said. "We're going to need whatever light you have available. Bullets need to be dug out and wounds sewed up."

Elizabeth nodded and tried to grab a shred of self-control. These men needed doctoring, and she couldn't allow her anger at Durango to cloud her skills and deny them help.

"You aren't going to run, are you, Doc?" Durango asked in a cold, determined tone. She could also detect the underlying pain he was trying to hide, too. Pain from the bullet she'd put into him.

Guilt swamped through her, and she shook her head. No, she wouldn't run. At least not yet. He let go of her, and she moved into action, spitting out orders for Durango to get the fire going in the fireplace so she could boil water for the utensils she'd need. She also instructed Landon to get Tyrell into the first bedroom to the right down the hallway. It was the biggest one and the one she and Durango had used when he'd been here.

Sweet mercy, he'd kept her hot and aroused when he'd lived here, and then later when Landon had come to live with them, her arousal had doubled. Elizabeth pushed aside those unwanted thoughts and hurried to grab some clean linen from a closet.

Chapter Two

An hour later, Elizabeth wiped the perspiration from her forehead with the back of her hand and gazed at the two men lying quietly on the bed. The one she hadn't been able to sleep in since Durango had left. A swell of emotions threatened to tear up her eyes, but she bit back the tears. She wouldn't let Durango see how much his leaving had affected her. She would need to stay focused on these men's injuries.

Landon, who she'd cared for dearly, partly due to the fact he'd tried to talk Durango out of joining the gang with him, appeared weak from loss of blood. The bullet had lodged in the fleshy part of his upper thigh, making him lose lots of blood. But the powerful way he'd carried her and tossed her onto the couch and then held her beneath his big body made her realize he was a very strong man, despite his wound. He would be fine given some rest.

Tyrell's wound was a bit more serious. He would require bed rest for a few days due to his wound. She'd found the bullet dangerously close to his left kidney, but thankfully it hadn't hit anything vital. He would be sore, and he'd been very lucky. Both men had been very lucky.

Stupid fools. Why couldn't they have found a more safe way to make a living? She knew why. There were no jobs to be found. Durango had been a mechanic. Since the world was in chaos due to the Catastrophe, and any type of machinery had fried, compliments of the solar flares, his job had disappeared literally overnight.

Durango was the least hurt of the three. He'd kept his mouth shut, thankfully, while she'd tried hard to ignore the wicked beating of her heart as her gaze snapped to and fro along the wide expanse of tanned muscles lacing all the men's chests and arms while she'd dug out the bullets.

Durango knew her fetish for muscles. How they turned her on so hard and so fast that he'd always joked about her exploding like a firecracker whenever muscles came into her view. She detected traces of pain glazing his eyes as he watched her from his perch on a wooden chair that he'd dragged close to the bed. She didn't think it was the physical pain. Maybe emotional pain? Had he missed her as much as she'd missed him?

No, he'd made his decision about leaving, and now he would have to live with it.

Unfortunately, now with the two men snoring softly in her bed, Durango didn't appear in the least bit sleepy as he studied her every move with his sultry light blue eyes. She could tell from the heated way he looked at her that he wanted sex. He always wanted sex, and in the past she'd loved losing herself in the pleasure he gave so easily. But she'd booted him out, and no matter how much she wanted him back in her bed, she needed to stick to her principles. Didn't she? Yes, she did, she added firmly.

"If you want to stay warm you'll have to crawl into bed between them," she snapped as she got up off the bed.

She reached out to grab the tray of bloody utensils, but he stopped her by grabbing her wrist, his fingers yet again snapping around her flesh like a handcuff.

She trembled at the strength in those fingers. Fingers that used to stroke so nicely in and out of her pussy. Fingers that caressed and brushed her nipples until they were on fire. Until she was on fire for him.

She gasped as he suddenly pulled her onto his lap. His arms came around her waist, and he held her in his strong, warm embrace. For a split second she thought about struggling out of his tight grasp, but she knew if he didn't want to let her go, he wouldn't, and fighting him would be a waste of time. She inhaled sharply at the feel of the large knot of arousal pressed against her ass. She could feel the pounding of his heart as it beat against her left arm. She also realized how easily and instinctively she was curling against him. That pissed her off.

Stupid woman. She couldn't give him the satisfaction of showing him how he still could so easily affect her.

He must have caught a glimpse of her mood, for he suddenly spoke softly in her ear. "I wonder what you'd do if I decided to kiss you, Doc?"

"Slap you," she retorted, injecting as much anger into her voice as she could.

"In that case I'd have to spank you. And I know how much you enjoy getting spanked, Doc."

"Don't call me that," Liz snapped.

"Does it bring back memories?"

Yes, his nickname, and his low, seductive voice and talk about spankings brought back those luscious memories. Too many memories. Of what he and his friend Landon had wanted to do with her before she'd sent them packing.

Warmth, unrestrained and wickedly delightful, whipped through her, and she could barely stop the breathless tremors as they raced through her tense body.

"It brings back nothing," she said coolly, but to her irritation she also sounded husky.

His knowing look angered her, and she forced herself to break his gaze. Wanting to escape him, she decided it would be better to fight him. To her surprise, when she did just that, he let her get up off his lap. She grabbed the tray containing the soiled utensils and stormed toward the door.

"Walking away won't stop what we both want, Liz." The softness in his voice almost undid her self-control, and she swore there was a brief hesitation in her walk, but she rectified it quickly by picking up her pace.

The bastard had nerve. She hadn't seen him in so long, and the last thing she wanted was to fall right back in love with him. She would not be shared by any man. No matter how often or how hot she got whenever she fantasized about having sex with him and other men. Sharing just wasn't normal. She'd do well to remember that fact.

* * * *

All you need to do is play it cool with her, Durango said to himself as he watched Doc walk out of the room. But looking at the sexy curve of her hips, and her perfectly shaped ass pressing intimately against her sweetly tight light green nightgown, made playing it cool damned hard.

Ethan Durango had a big problem, and her name was Dr. Elizabeth Brandywine. He'd forced himself to stay away from her after their last argument when she'd given him two ultimatums. Never speak about his sexual desires regarding sharing her again and don't join the Durango Gang. Hell, if he'd agreed to her terms, she may as well have castrated him. The last thing he wanted was to be tied down like a caged dog and made to feel as useless as one.

Over the months he thought he'd managed to get her out of his system, but of course those lonely, cold nights on the trail with a posse breathing up their asses had made him bring out a photo that he carried on him. A picture he'd shared with the members of the gang. The guys were pretty good where Liz was concerned. They looked at her picture, commented on her pretty blue eyes and her luscious strawberry-red lips or her sexy pose for the shot.

He knew Landon and Tyrell would be the men to share her with. Not because he wasn't threatened by them. He wasn't, but he knew both men were trustworthy, dependable, and both had been married. Watching their wives disintegrate right before their eyes during the solar flares had hardened them to love, but he saw the caring in their eyes when they'd looked at Liz's picture, and he just knew these were the men he wanted to stand by her with him.

With violence rampant these days, he knew it was just a matter of time before Liz was discovered living alone way out here in the middle of nowhere where she chose to practice her trade. He would have preferred her in a city, but cities were probably more dangerous without a man.

Looking out for her was why he made it a habit to send most of the injured members of the gang to her to recuperate. He'd also sent any member wanting access to a decent pleasure girl because Dr. Liz would check each man thoroughly. If he appeared to be in good health and wasn't carrying diseases, she would give him a name of a professional girl he could spend some time with. Those were a couple of ways he'd been able to keep tabs on her.

He hadn't planned on coming back to their century-old stone house for a little while longer, but when the gang had been in a shootout trying to rob a bank in a city on the other side of the mountains, Durango had brought them to the closest trusted doctor he knew, Doc.

Now that he was here, hopefully he could win himself back into her graces. Wishful thinking? Maybe. The moment he'd seen her again, all the self-control he'd wrapped tightly around himself had unraveled. He wanted to be back in her bed. Wanted to crack that icy exterior she valiantly tried to portray.

He'd caught glimpses of tenderness splashing across her face as she'd dug out the bullet in his arm. Felt the erotic way she'd melted against him when he'd dragged her into his lap, and yeah, he'd heard her sharp inhalation of breath as her ass came down on his thick erection.

She still loved him, and she loved the way her body reacted when she was around him. A hot love like theirs couldn't die. He sensed it would only grow if Liz could admit her deepest sexual needs to herself. All he needed to do was hold his self-control just a little harder.

They were such an odd couple. He was a blue-collar worker earning a living as a farm machinery mechanic, living on the outskirts of Calgary, Alberta. Doc had been a respectable family doctor. They probably would have never met if he hadn't sliced his palm open while working on a piece of equipment and she hadn't been gassing up her SUV at the self-serve gas pumps right outside the garage. She'd said she liked the rough sound of his voice when he'd cursed and watched him wrap his hand in a dirty rag. Her doctor side had been concerned, yet she'd said it had been the sight of his muscles that lured her into the dark garage. To him.

Durango smiled. Thank God for his muscles. Of course muscles had been another reason why he'd picked Tyrell and Landon. They were loaded with them. Strong men. They would give Liz plenty of pleasure on the long, cold nights here.

Perhaps he was being naïve in thinking she'd spread her thighs for them just because he'd brought home a couple of guys with big muscles. He knew she wasn't that much of a pushover. He wanted her to embrace her desires. Not do it because it pleased him. Although, he knew she wouldn't submit, unless it was right for her. He just wished she wasn't taking such a long time in figuring it out. She was the strongest yet shiest woman he'd ever met. Her strength and her confidence in her work made her sexy to him. Her shyness in the bedroom made her even more sexy.

Damn him. What had he expected her to do when he'd plopped her into his lap earlier anyway? That she'd wrap her arms around his neck and welcome him back into her bed like the old days before the Catastrophe? Back then they'd been engaged. He'd suppressed his sexual urges and the urge to explore their sex life. Ignored his craving to share her with other men.

She'd called him a sexual deviant when he'd told her he fantasized about sharing her. He shouldn't have expected any different reaction than when he'd left her. She was still the same sexually uptight doctor he'd fallen in love with. She was still in denial about her needs and her fantasies. He knew she fantasized because he'd listened to her soft, sultry moans while she'd slept. He'd heard her mutter his friends' names. Her erotic moans always turned him on, and sometimes he fucked her while she'd slept. Yeah, sexual deviant. She'd hit the nail on the head with those two words regarding him.

"Your first fight, and you haven't even been back a couple of hours." Amusement laced Tyrell's voice from where he lay on the bed. Durango turned to look down at his friend and breathed a sigh of relief. His brown eyes didn't seem as glazed with pain, and he swore he didn't look as pale anymore either.

"The more we fight, the better we make up."

Tyrell chuckled, winced, held his side, and fell silent.

"So, how do you feel?" Durango asked.

"Better. Looking at your beautiful woman helped."

Warmth shifted through him at his compliment of Liz.

Beside Tyrell, he noticed Landon was also awake. His green eyes gazed back at him, and he was smiling. Obviously the two had been playing possum so Durango could spend some alone time with Doc. Crazy guys.

"I hope so," Landon replied. "Because I haven't had a woman in a long time, and just looking at her has me painfully rock hard."

Durango grinned. "And I like the way you get straight to the point, my man. Now get some sleep. You both need to get your strength back. The doc likes it rough and hard," he teased, then laughed as both Landon and Tyrell moaned and cursed at him.

Yeah, Doc liked it rough and hard, but she also liked it tender and gentle. The three of them could do both. Being back in their home, he wasn't going to let her deny what they both needed this time. This time around he was going to break through those walls she held up regarding her sexual fantasies and he'd have her wanting all three of them, and he would be doing it sooner rather than later.

* * * *

Elizabeth knew Durango wouldn't leave her alone for long. When he wanted something, he worked fast. He'd always been that way. If he wanted sex, he was like a dog with a bone. His persistence was what drew her to him. She was like a helpless moth drawn to the dangerous, dark flame. That was exactly how she was feeling now as she placed her disinfected doctoring tools back into her black bag and listened to the floorboards creak beneath Durango's heavy weight as he stepped into the living room where she'd sequestered herself on the fireplace outer hearth.

She didn't want to fall into his arms. Didn't want him to go away again either. Truth be told, she was confused. Mystified at why she loved him so much yet hated what he wanted from her. Perhaps hated was too strong a word. Maybe a better word would be denial, just as Durango had always said.

She focused her attention to zipping up the black bag and then placing it on the coffee table before turning to stare into the flickering fire. The orange-yellow flare of flames reminded her of their relationship. Intense, right from the moment she'd laid eyes on him. It had been in that dirty, humid garage, muscles galore bunching in his grease-streaked arms and sweaty chest as he wrapped his injured hand in a filthy rag, all the while cursing at some odd-looking piece of machinery perched precariously on the cement floor, when he'd caught her full attention.

He'd been shirtless big-time that day, and she swore her muscle fetish had started right then and there. Yeah, sure she'd reacted seeing other men without shirts, but they hadn't smelled sexy and sweaty like Durango.

"Do you still dream about us, Liz?" he asked as if knowing exactly what she was thinking. He'd moved closer now. Stood right beside her. She could feel his body heat. It was hotter than the waves of heat coming off the fire. She'd always reacted that way to him.

She'd almost literally latched herself to him that first time in the garage, too. Of course her concern for the blood-soaked dirty rag he'd wound around his hand had won out. She'd taken him to a local clinic where a doctor friend of hers worked, and he'd tended Durango's deep gash, stitching it up perfectly. After that, Durango had invited her out for coffee. She'd accepted, and then they'd gone to his place, where she'd simply given into her sexual desire for him while they'd showered and fucked. She'd never lost her control to a stranger before. She had never done it with anyone else since.

She wanted to tell him that, yes, she dreamed about him every night. Dreamed about the sex with him and with other men. She didn't tell him that fact. She had her pride.

"I dream about us every night," he whispered. "I dream about how it used to be. How it will be."

Irritation snapped through her. My, oh my, he had confidence in himself where she was concerned, didn't he?

She would have gotten up off the hearth if he hadn't been standing right there behind her, sandwiching her between him and the fire. Suddenly she felt hot and weak with desire, waiting for him to touch her.

"I dream about taking you right here in front of this fire." His soft voice stroked over her nerves like melting chocolate. She creamed in her panty and tried hard to ignore the insistent throb of need burning deep inside her pussy as visions of him sliding his cock into her erupted in her mind.

She swallowed and cleared her throat. "I'm afraid I don't feel anything more for you, Durango. I still stand at what was said before you left. You made your decision." Oh, but the sultry sound of her voice certainly was saying different. She knew he would be able to hear the lie, too.

She inhaled softly as his hand curled over her shoulder, and she swore any resolve she had toward him went right up the chimney with the smoke.

"I want you, baby. I've wanted you every night since I've been gone."

Damn him.

"Then you shouldn't have left, should you?" she bit out. "Because now it's too late."

"It's never too late between us. Unless you've taken on a lover or two while I've been gone?"

He studied her for a reaction. She tried hard not to blink. Fought for the control she knew she would need because he always knew when she was lying. She definitely did not want to give away that she'd had no other man in her bed since he'd been gone.

"That is none of your business."

"Well, it is my business, Doc, because you see, I've invested a lot of time in looking for the perfect men to share you with."

Oh God. She was really creaming now. Not good.

"I already told you—"

"Your body language says different, Liz. I can read you like a book, baby. I was watching you when you were tending Landon and Tyrell. Watching how your gaze kept snapping to their muscles. How your hands shook with the need to touch them."

Bastard. So he was right. It didn't mean she wanted them in her bed. Despite her denial, her vagina spasmed, her ass pulsed, and naughty images of the three men ruthlessly fucking her filled her head. She found herself inhaling deeply to steady her sudden panic.

She was totally helpless as Durango's hand curled around her shoulder. He told her to scoot over a couple of feet until her back was now against the cool stone wall of the fireplace. Now she was facing forward toward him, her legs over the edge of the outer hearth.

Oh darn it, he hadn't bothered to put his shirt on, and the orange firelight danced crazily over rippling muscles galore as his fingers flexed on her shoulder. The white linen she'd wrapped around his injury shone like a beacon in the gloomy early morning light, and it made his flesh look scrumptiously tanned. She'd always warned him against going shirtless due to the dangers of skin cancer, but obviously he hadn't listened. He was so darkly tanned, and he looked so good. So healthy. Being a member of the Durango Gang obviously agreed with him.

Hot flames blasted against her right side from the fire in the fireplace, and she became mesmerized as she watched his fingers trail from her shoulder and his hands drop over her knees and slowly part her thighs.

"I haven't been with a woman since I left you," he whispered, his voice thick with lust.

He hadn't slept with others? Durango was a very sensual man who enjoyed sex every night and many times during the days as well. Not having had any sex in months…he—she swallowed as a cyclone of erotic shivers raced through her—he would be a bundle of unexploded energy.

"Landon hasn't been with a woman either. Neither has Tyrell, since I selected him for you. For them, it's been months as well. They crave sex on a regular basis as I do. They've been ready to take you for too long."

She wanted to tell Durango he was dreaming for thinking she would sleep with the men he'd brought home. Somehow, she couldn't utter a protest. Could only fight to keep her breaths steady as his meaning hit home.

Three men with extreme pent-up sexual energy wanted her. If he hadn't been holding her knees wide open, she would have closed them and brought herself off at the mere thought of three men touching her, all at the same time. Of their mouths kissing her in intimate places. Of them bringing her fantasies of being triple penetrated to life.

His hands tightened on her knees, and she swore her breaths halted in her lungs as he kneeled down on his haunches in front of her, between her parted thighs. He gazed up at her with those lust-laden eyes, and she became lost in his heated look. Just like that. Oh, damn him for being so bold and sexy. For forcing her to confront her desires for him and the fantasies they both shared.

"We can go slow. Just you and me to start," he said softly. "We can get reacquainted. Right here. Right now." It seemed as if he were giving her a way out in the manner he posed his sentences. She didn't want a way out. She wanted him to push her past her restraints.

Oh goodness, she couldn't believe she'd just thought that last thought.

"Lower your nightgown." His hoarse voice had her trembling despite the heat pumping out of the hearth. The thought of what he wanted to do had her nipples hardening and peeking and pressing boldly against her nightgown.

"Durango…" She didn't know what she wanted to say. Maybe she wanted to mount a protest? No, no, she wanted him to touch her, kiss her, and fuck her. Not necessarily in that order.

He continued to gaze at her from his perch between her spread legs. His eyes were a dusty blue, and she swore she'd never seen them that dark before. Or so filled with sensuality and arousal. That look made her yearn for him so badly it almost pushed her senses into overdrive.

"Can you imagine Landon and Tyrell thrusting inside you? I know I want to see the pleasure splash across your face when they do. I know you've fantasized about Landon. I heard you call his name many times in your sleep before I left."

Damn him. He'd never told her *that* before. Yes, she had fantasized about Landon. Who couldn't? The man looked so hot, and he was built just as gorgeously as Durango, and he was so sweet, too.

"Have you already fantasized about Tyrell while you were patching him up?"

She found herself shaking her head despite the fact she had been ogling his taut, tanned torso while she'd prodded past his tattered flesh looking for the bullet.

"Now why don't you pull that nightie down so I can see more of you, Doc? I've wanted to touch you since the moment I left. I've missed you like crazy."

She shook her head, but at the same time her heart hammered insanely against her chest as she held his intoxicating gaze, and she lifted her hands. He licked his lips in obvious anticipation as she slowly eased the straps of her nightgown down her arms and then dipped her hands beneath the lowered neckline. She drew out her breasts both at the same time, presenting herself to him.

Her breaths halted as Durango swore softly. Appreciation lit his eyes, and lust flushed his face a nice shade of pink. Hunger tensed his body.

"Yeah, just the way I remember them. Nice, very nice, baby."

She jerked as his hands pressed against her knees and he moved himself forward between her spread legs, his upper body leaning closer to her, his lips parting. She became lost in the sexy curve of those lips as his hot breath lashed her left nipple. As he sucked her taut flesh right into his searing, moist mouth, she shuddered uncontrollably. Oh, to have him at her breast again. It felt so right.

Reaching out with both of her hands, her arms arched around his neck. Her fingers sifted through the shoulder-length strands of his dark, silky brown hair where she gently held him. She gasped as the wonderful ripples of arousal began to build deep inside her pussy. The incredible way he sucked intoxicated her. Heated her.

She twisted against him, arching her back so she could get a firmer pressure. She could hear him breathing harshly. Heard herself moaning softly, giving herself away that she was enjoying what he was doing to her.

Damn him, he was like a fever rushing through her system. A fever chasing and exposing her deepest desires, her most wanton needs. He'd always been like this.

He demanded, she submitted, because, well, quite truthfully, she enjoyed the way he made her feel. Just as he was doing now.

Bastard.

He let go of her nipple with a pop and moved to her other breast, sucking her other nipple into his mouth. His teeth grazed back and forth, igniting fiery pleasure-pain. His tongue soothed as he smoothed over her tortured flesh. Her pussy creamed. Her mind shattered, and she lost all self-control. Her body tightened, the ache for penetration spreading quickly through her body. Perspiration dotted her skin. Her breasts felt swollen and the rest of her overwhelmed and needy.

"Damn you, Durango," she whispered as she creamed and almost came. He could do that, make her come by sucking on her nipples, but the son of a bitch obviously didn't want her to come yet. She moaned in protest as he drew his head away and glared up at her.

"Maybe I should just leave you like this, huh, Liz? Give you a little taste of what I've been going through all these months."

Selfish, wasn't he? Thinking he was the only one who'd been suffering. *Well, screw him. Let him think it.* She wouldn't beg him to take her. She wouldn't!

Despite thinking that she wouldn't give into him, her hands curled with frustration into tight fists of restraint behind his neck. She craved to bring her hands down to press against her pussy and make herself climax. She knew she would be able to. He'd brought her *that* close. To her irritation, he smiled knowingly.

"No, I shouldn't deny myself. Shouldn't leave you like this."

Reaching up, he grabbed her arms and slowly brought them down to her sides. "Keep them there. Don't touch me."

She whimpered at his sharp command and did as he told her, watching helplessly as his hands moved her nightie up and past her knees, then her hips. His breaths came faster, harsher, as cool air pushed against her nude pussy.

Yes, she was nude down there. She'd had herself permanently denuded shortly after going out with Durango. He'd wanted her that way, and she hadn't seen any reason to deny him. Just like now. She couldn't deny him. Couldn't stop herself from wanting his mouth on her down there.

God, she was so *weak*.

Once again her helplessness and her defiance made her watch as he got into position, his head lowering to between her spread legs. She widened herself, silently begging, mutely urging him to hurry. Praying he wasn't going to stop and just walk away.

She jerked wildly as his shoulders pushed her wider. His fingers slipped against her pussy, and he parted her outer labia. Then she cried out, dazed at the intoxicating intensity, as his tongue lashed her amazingly responsive clit like a frantic whip. Sensations zapped through her. Intense. Explosive. And when he plunged three fingers into her soaked vagina—

She came. Hard.

She whimpered, her thighs clenching against him as she tried to clamp them shut. But his broad shoulders prevented it. She cried out as his tongue kissed and licked her clit and his fingers plunged in and out of her as if they were a miniature cock. Arousal rocked her, making her hips wrench this way and that way. Making her pant furiously and clench her fists tighter as he went down on her full force. She could feel her juices seeping like a river down her channel, hot and moist. She could hear the suctioning sound of his fingers thrusting in and out and mingling with his erotic groans and her sultry moans.

He didn't stop. He kept up the pressure with his mouth, his tongue kissing and licking her clit, and his fingers thrusting into her wet vagina. She just kept creaming for him, her back arching against him, pressing herself into his face. She loved the harsh brush of his whiskers as they erotically caressed the insides of her thighs.

God! Would this exquisite torture ever end?

The moment she found herself coming down from a climax, he would increase his thrusts as well as the pressure on her clit, until he forced her into another orgasm. By the time he was finished, perspiration drenched her nightgown and she was utterly exhausted. If he'd decided to call the other two men to join him she would have been too tired to protest. Too exhausted to do anything but lay back and let them wrench even more arousal from her parched and spent body.

"There, that's the way I like to see you, Doc. Utterly satisfied. Your gorgeous eyes half lidded, your pussy red and swollen and eagerly awaiting more."

He was right. Oh, the man was so right. She wanted to be taken again, despite the exhaustion clinging to her. Her pussy felt so wonderfully swollen and used. Achy and simply ready to be taken over and over again.

She thought for sure he would finish this by taking her hands and leading her to the couch where he would fuck her again and they would sleep together, like the old days.

To her disappointment, he didn't. Instead he stood and looked down at her, his face twisted with lust and torment.

"If you want more of this, Doc, you'll have to wear a plug so you can be stretched and then Landon and Tyrell can take you."

Oh damn him! Damn him for doing this to her!

"Go to hell, Durango," she spat in a fierce whisper. She would have yelled at him, had she the strength.

He shook his head, an odd smile tilting those sensuously shaped lips of his.

"Honey, without you, I'm there."

Having said that, he walked away, his confident swagger snapping anger through her like a live wire. She swore if she'd had the energy, she would have grabbed something, anything, and thrown it at him.

It took every ounce of her being to stand. Her legs wobbled weakly from the onslaught of climaxes he'd given her, and she could barely make it to the couch where she practically fell onto the soft cushions. Tugging at the comforters, she wrapped herself in them like a cocoon and slept like she'd never slept before.

Chapter Three

"You're looking like the cat that ate the canary." Tyrell grinned as Durango stepped back into the bedroom where Ty and Landon were sequestered. In the old days having two men lying leisurely on a bed together meant comments about them being gay. But these days, men huddled together all the time for warmth. Modesty and friendly jokes were quickly forgotten.

"Move your ass over so I can climb in, and I just might tell you how sweet our canary tastes."

Both Tyrell and Landon blinked up at him, their mouths parting in shock as his meaning came across. They both swore softly, and they grimaced in pain as they moved and disrupted their injuries. They gave him more room than he needed.

Dropping his jeans, both men whistled as his painful erection boldly pressed against his underwear.

"Fuck, my man, what did you do to deserve that?" Landon chuckled.

"More like what didn't you do to deserve that," Tyrell said, shaking his head. "She must be some fantastic chick."

"If you two hadn't gotten yourself shot up so bad, then you might have been able to partake in the pleasures. But, alas, lucky I, for taking only a flesh wound." Durango winked at them, and they cursed him down.

"You shouldn't have made her believe she was the one who'd shot you," Landon said softly as the three settled beneath the covers.

"Yeah, that wasn't nice. When the lie comes out, and it will, she's going to be doubly pissed off." Tyrell grumbled.

"At all three of us, because you two had plenty of opportunity to speak up and set me straight. Now you are my accomplices and thus will harbor her wrath when she learns the truth," Durango quipped, trying to hide his smile as he teased the guys and they once again cursed him down.

"Yep, she did taste very good. Too bad you two are so badly shot."

"Durango," Landon said, and Durango could hear the warning in his voice to stop.

"You're torturing us, my man," Tyrell replied in a cool tone.

"Sorry, guys, sweet dreams. I know I'll certainly have them."

He closed his eyes and smiled as the other two men shifted uneasily, obviously getting very uncomfortable as their imaginations ran wild about what he'd been doing with Liz.

Good. They should be miserable, because misery, meaning him, loved company at the moment.

* * * *

She couldn't believe she let Durango go down on her after he'd only been in her home for a couple of hours. He'd been gone for months. How dare he come back into her life and think he could just start having sex with her. She didn't want to be sucked into what he wanted from her. Didn't want to become a sex toy to him and his friends. Where would it stop? Would it go beyond three men? Although that idea terrified her, it also aroused her.

God, was she ever screwed up!

During her last visit, her nearest neighbor, Teyla Sutton, had confided to Liz that since being with three men at the same time, Teyla didn't dream of going back to having sex on a regular basis with just one man. She simply enjoyed ménages too much.

Is that what would happen to her? Would she lose herself in the pleasure of three men?

Liz bit back a sob. She wanted her old life back. It had been so simple back then. One man who'd loved her, family, and the conveniences of civilization, which included a phone and electricity, running hot water and an abundance of food.

Instead, she was freezing her butt off out here. She stood naked, her bare feet wobbling on rocks in the cold water of a river that ran through her property, and she had the most picturesque scenery of snowcapped craggy mountains in the distance while she washed herself. Her teeth chattered so loudly she wouldn't be surprised if her closest neighbors heard her two miles away.

She sighed and dipped a bucket of water into the cold water. Bringing it up over her head, she held her breath and tipped it, gasping and cursing as the liquid practically froze her sensitive skin as it washed over her.

Sweet mercy! But that water was cold!

Dropping the pail, she grabbed the face cloth she'd placed on a nearby boulder and dipped it into the water before generously soaping the cloth. Normally she would have lugged in some buckets of water from the well outside her house and warmed it in the cast-iron pot she kept hanging over the fire in the living room fireplace. But she didn't want Durango and his friends walking in on her while she washed her intimate parts. Parts that were exquisitely tender after Durango had had his way with her.

She held her breath as she splayed the cold, soapy washcloth over her right breast. Talk about freezing! She'd hoped the cold water would distinguish the heat of arousal flaring through her body since she'd woken from her nap after Durango had left her spent. But the cold air breathing against her moist flesh, and now the water dribbling erotically over her fevered skin, only seemed to heighten her senses and awareness that sleeping in her bed were three very sexy, well-muscled men.

When she'd awoken, the house had been too quiet and panic had sawed through her like a painful blade as she'd wondered if Durango and the others had left once again. Her uneasiness had only increased as she'd rushed down the hallway. Holding her breath, she'd pushed open the doorway to her bedroom, and thankfully they'd still been there. The three of them were fast asleep, their soft snores zipping through the cool air.

She'd watched them.

The new man, Tyrell Mathews, looked exquisitely handsome as he slept, his long, dark eyelashes framing his cheeks. His hair was dark brown, and he had a short, military-style cut. He was as darkly tanned as Durango, and he'd smelled very nice. While she'd tended to his wound, he'd kept quiet, his dark brown eyes studying her. Whenever he'd answered her questions, he'd answered in a mannerly tone which gave her the impression he was sweet and nice. Durango had been right though. Tyrell's muscles certainly had made her insides twist about in an erotic way. Damn Durango for bringing another muscle-bound man into her home and into her life.

Landon Leigh's light coloring was in direct contrast to Durango's dark coloring. Where Durango had shoulder-length straight dark brown, almost-black hair and dark blue eyes, Landon's hair was just as long and straight, but light sandy brown, almost blond, with green eyes. All three of them were big men, heavily muscled with dark five-o'clock shadows hugging their cheeks and chin.

They were sexy, dangerous desperadoes who were wanted by the law. Well, not that there was a legitimate law around these days. Vigilantes, people who'd taken it upon themselves to protect others or use their power over vulnerable people, preferred to hang people, before asking questions.

Lately the Durango Gang was on the top of their hit list, with their pictures on wanted posters all over town. They were a gang who robbed from the rich and gave to the poor, the rich meaning people who made extremely high profits off the misery of others.

Liz didn't have a problem with the Durango Gang. These days lawlessness ran rampant, and one had to do anything to survive. She just wished Durango hadn't decided to run with such a crowd that seemed to get shot up almost every time they did a bank heist or some other sort of robbery. Making enemies of the rich people was never a good thing.

The entire time Durango and Landon had been gone, she'd worried for their safety. She had inquired after them whenever one or more of the Durango members came to her for a referral to a pleasure girl or if they were injured. That was how she'd kept tabs on them.

She knew Landon wanted her. Durango had told her that shortly before they'd left. And Durango had wanted to share her with him. She liked the man. Okay, so just looking at him made her pussy pulse and her breasts yearn for him to touch her, but that didn't mean she had to sleep with the guy. At least it hadn't been required of her before the entire world had gone mad, including Durango.

Her gaze had then settled on Durango, the man she'd once called her heart. He did look much better than when he'd left, she had to admit. Before he'd gone away he'd possessed the look of a caged animal. Dark circles had hung beneath his eyes, and furrows had appeared at the sides of his mouth, compliments of a constant frown.

She realized now that she hadn't been good enough for him. She'd wanted to be, but she wasn't. He'd wanted more out of life than just settling down and trying to survive. He'd wanted to make a difference in this new world. Apparently, for him, joining the Robin Hood-style gang was the ticket.

Liz frowned and combed her fingers through her wet hair. Well, perhaps he'd gotten his adventurous streak out of his system and had come home to be with her? Yeah, right. Wishful thinking. He was probably here because she'd been convenient to patch up Landon and Tyrell and the three of them wanted some hot sex before taking off on her again. And it was at that exact moment she'd realized she didn't want to fight with Durango anymore. She was holding onto an old way of life that would never come back. She hated change, but she now realized that changing and adapting to this new environment was the only way she would have a chance at being happy again.

Why should she deny herself the pleasures that Durango and his two friends wanted to give to her? Since the Catastrophe everything had become distorted. Why not live a few hot fantasies while she was still alive?

In town, she'd heard gossip that the environment may get even colder. God forbid if that happened. People were having trouble keeping any outdoor crops alive, let alone trying to grow feed for livestock that could be ultimately butchered for meat.

Times had gotten harsh since the Catastrophe. All of her family and extended family must have been wiped out. She'd never gone back East to find out. How could she? Nothing was running. No trains, no buses, no planes.

The only way back would be on one of those pioneer wagon trains that some people were signing up for. Caravans or something like that. Just like in the Old West days.

No, it was best to stay put. She knew if one of her three brothers or her parents had survived they would have come looking for her. She'd sent several letters back recently through what they were calling "The Pony Express," named after the original Pony Express that the United States had had back in 1849 where riders rode all day and all night to get mail from East to West and vice versa.

The price for the Pony Express service was steep, and because most people didn't have a job anymore, they didn't pay her money for her doctoring services. Instead of giving her money, they gave her food or handmade items.

The lavender-scented soap she washed herself with had been a gift from one of her patients, a little old lady whom Elizabeth knew only by the name of Sally. She lived alone in the next valley. Obviously no pensions existed anymore, so she'd been cut off.

Sally's entire family had disintegrated in the solar flares, and Sally had found herself totally alone and fending for herself. She hadn't sobbed in the middle of a river like Elizabeth was doing herself. The old woman had accepted the change, and she'd gone into the soap-making business in order to survive. If Sally could survive without looking back, then Liz should be able to do it, too, right? Right. Liz firmly nodded and inhaled sharply as she washed off the soap and quickly soaped her shoulder-length blonde hair.

Bending over to grab the pail so she could rinse the soap from her hair, she sucked in a breath as cold water touched her tender pussy. The lapping of liquid evoked all kinds of naughty images of what had happened early this morning with Durango's face buried between her spread thighs.

Oh boy, she was in so much trouble here just thinking of Durango and of why he'd brought Landon and Tyrell back with him. She swallowed as her ass clenched with anticipation when she remembered Durango warning her if she wanted more she'd need to wear a butt plug.

She had plugs in the bedroom drawer where the three men slept. She'd used them when she'd been with Durango. Used them a lot. And if he got his way she'd be wearing them again. Probably more than ever.

Erotic heat zipped through her, and she blew out a tense breath. Okay, she needed to get out of the water and stop thinking about him and the other men. She needed to do it now, or with the intoxicating way the water stroked her clit, she'd begin masturbating.

She didn't want to do that. Not with three men sleeping in her house, and who knew if they'd followed her out here and were watching her right now while she bathed. That thought both alarmed and excited her as she cast a fast glance at her surroundings.

From where she stood, she saw nothing but rain-dampened bushes lining both sides of the river. Here and there a bird chirped, and the ever-present cold wind whipped through the bare branches. Even the bushes and trees were barely surviving. Leaves still came out, but they didn't look as green and lush as they once did. They appeared gnarled with a yellowing, sickly tinge. Everything looked dreary in the valley now. Despite the rain and clouds moving out of the area, the sun had come out. But it was still cold. The sun always came out and kept on shining as if nothing had ever happened.

Biting back a bitter sob, she rinsed her hair and then splashed herself, making sure all the soap was cleaned away before she hurriedly stumbled out of the river. Gathering the fresh pair of clothes she'd laid on some bushes in the sunshine, she quickly slipped into a pair of black leggings and a warm, wool, knee-length, tunic-style wraparound dress. Sliding on her warm brown leather jacket, Liz began to feel much warmer as the clothing chased away her shivers. Before long, her chattering teeth had stopped, and she was feeling back to her old self again.

Taking a deep breath, she gazed at the stone house nestled about a quarter of a mile away. Most of the roof was covered in a green moss, and wild vines clung to the stone walls. To any passerby the place would look serene. Maybe even deserted. Little did they know she had three fugitives lying fast asleep in her bed.

Three sexy desperadoes who wanted to be with *her*. *Have mercy*, she was beginning to feel terribly warm again just thinking about the things she wanted them to do to her. She ignored the gush of warm cream seeping from between her thighs. She would have to be strong now. She would have to stick to her morals no matter how much she craved to explore this sharing thing that Durango wanted. Elizabeth swallowed and started walking toward the house and toward her destiny.

* * * *

She was coming up the well-trodden trail that meandered through the yellowing grass of the nearby meadow. Landon watched the lone feminine figure walking leisurely toward the stone house. He'd taken sentry beside the bedroom window shortly after hearing her leave an hour or so earlier. Pushing aside the dainty white lace curtains, he'd watched her sweet hips swaying and her shoulder-length, honey-gold hair waving in the wind as she'd strolled across the yellowing field. She'd been carrying a pink towel, so he knew she'd been heading down to the river to bathe.

Brandy. He liked that name on her. His nickname for her, because her hair looked just like the color of golden brandy when the sun hit it, and heck, with her last name of Brandywine, that name just fit.

The sun was hitting her hair that way right now as she strolled closer, the golden blonde strands waving like spun gold drying in the wind. He remembered from his previous stay here that she liked to air-dry her hair while going on solitary walks after bathing.

She looked really pretty. Even prettier than when he and Durango had left to join his cousin's gang. She even reminded him a little of his wife, Betty. She'd been a blonde, too, and they'd been so in love and recently married when the Catastrophe had come calling. Betty and he had been at her parents' house over in Calgary when the solar flares had flashed against the windows.

He'd thought it had been lightning, and he'd looked toward one window, his gaze leaving his startled wife one final time, his hand letting go of her hand as he thought about getting up to go and see what was going on.

At the same time he'd heard moans from around the table where he'd been sitting with his wife, her parents, and her two sisters, sharing the news that Betty was four months pregnant with twins.

One minute they'd been there, the next minute flashes of fire, grey smoke, and a really bad smell of burning flesh had burst through the dining room. When he'd swung his head to look, thinking maybe some sort of gas explosion had occurred, the woman he loved and her family had been piles of smoking grey ashes on their seats.

A really cold, creepy feeling slithered through Landon at remembering how he'd been stunned for hours afterwards. How the icy goose bumps had scattered along his arms and lasted for months after that day. He preferred not to think about that day. Preferred not to relive it.

Hell, he still had lots of nightmares about it. Still had lots of dreams of what life might have been like with Betty still alive and with two toddlers running around following him while he did the household chores. He pushed the anger and the despair back down inside himself where it belonged. He figured it was best not to ponder on it during daylight hours. Nights, he had no control over.

Instead, he preferred to focus on Brandy. She was his future. Their new future. He would protect her with his life. He would protect their children. That is, if she agreed to having a couple kids with him. He didn't want her to think she was a baby-making machine, but yeah, he'd dreamed of having a couple of kids. Maybe it was some weird twisted dream to replace the two he'd lost? He hoped not.

Truthfully, he had probably fallen in love with her the minute he'd seen her when Durango had brought him home from Heart Creek, the nearest town where he'd been looking for work. He'd been half starved, and he'd been willing to work for food and a roof over his head. Durango had said he and Liz had just moved into the old place and that it needed fixing up big-time. He'd said they'd picked the quaint century-old home because it was the sturdiest abandoned building they'd come across and it was far away from the chaos of town, yet not so far that people who needed doctoring couldn't find them.

Yeah, he'd liked her right from the start. Liz was a tall woman. Thin with curves in all the right places.

While working around the house he'd seen that look of interest flare in her pale blue eyes when she thought he didn't see. But he also knew interest didn't mean she wanted sack time with him. It was very obvious she was in love with Durango, and so he'd watched the two lovebirds and had tried hard to remain neutral. Had managed fine until that day Durango had told him he wanted to share Liz.

With him.

That's when his old world had shattered and his new world had been born. Unfortunately he was still the one on the outside looking in. He wanted to change that, but he didn't want to make the move. It would have to come from Durango or Liz herself because she knew she had Durango's blessing.

As she neared, he noticed her stiffen, and as if sensing she was being watched, she snapped her head up and gazed directly at him.

Shit. Too late to move from the window. He'd been caught.

Hesitantly she lifted her arm and waved. She smiled, and his heart warmed at the sight. She looked really pretty when she smiled, especially when her dimples exploded in her cheeks like they were doing now. He didn't waste any time in waving back.

A couple of minutes later he heard the front door open as she entered. The hinges creaked as they had early this morning when they'd arrived. Durango had knocked the signal they used, not too loudly because he hadn't wanted to frighten her if she'd been home and asleep. But he said she would recognize his knock, and if she wasn't still really pissed off, she would answer. She hadn't answered. Upon discovering her horse wasn't around, Durango had thought maybe she'd gone to visit a client or maybe she'd moved out altogether.

Although, her moving from this place hadn't been too likely, because before coming here, Durango, Tyrell, and he had visited Landon's brother Logan where he now lived with two men at a farmhouse on the other side of this valley. They said they'd spoken to Liz only a couple of weeks ago, and everything had been fine then.

Logan and two other gang members had given up the gang for a cute pleasure girl they'd taken a shine to. Landon had to admit she was a very nice-looking woman and very pleasant to talk to. Seeing his brother happy and settling into farm life made him want to settle down, too. With Liz.

He hoped Durango and Tyrell were on the same wavelength. Although he didn't know exactly how they could swing it with a vigilante wanting to hang them. It would most definitely be a problem. But since there was no real law to speak of, they could surely work around any potential mob by shooting at them and forcing them off the property.

He could hear Liz moving around in the kitchen. Could hear some pots clanging and knew she would set upon making something for everyone to eat. She was like that—enjoyed cooking—and Landon had never gone hungry when he'd lived here.

On the bed, Tyrell and Durango stirred, and their movement prompted Landon to hobble away from the window. Thankfully, the bed was so close that he didn't have to put pressure on his bad leg more than a couple of times, because his thigh was still pretty sore, and most likely would be for some days to come. He should lie down and go back to sleep. Rest. Get reenergized for when the time came to take Liz.

"You should go out and talk to her. Get reacquainted." Durango's sleepy voice zipped through the air, making Landon tense. It still felt odd sometimes thinking that Durango had agreed to share his girl with him. And that Durango wanted to share her with Ty, too. Not that Landon had a problem with sharing. He and his wife had been swingers. That's how they'd met, at a swingers club.

Throughout their relationship he'd shared his wife with other men. That's how he'd known Liz would be acceptable of it. She had the same twinkle of curiosity in her eyes as his wife, Betty. But Betty and he had been confident in their relationship. They enjoyed swinging and having sex with others. But at the end of each session, they knew they belonged to each other and went home together, to their own bed.

"She needs time to get used to the idea," Landon replied, grimacing back a shard of pain that zipped through his wounded thigh as he slipped back under the comforters beside Ty, who still slept.

"She's had months to get used to the idea," Durango said. "Deep down inside of her, she knew I'd eventually come back. She was pissed off back then, and it clouded her needs. She's ready. I know it. I know her."

Landon nodded. Yes, Durango knew her, and Landon knew her as well. She was ready. She just needed to be pushed.

"What about after we recuperate? After we take her? We can't just leave her here, like before. Something is going to happen to her. We can't have somebody protecting her all the time while we're gone. It would have to be one of us. Someone we trust." *Like me*, Landon replied silently. He hadn't told Durango that he would quit the gang before he left Liz on her own again.

Sure, they had his brother, Logan, dropping in and keeping tabs on her. Durango, as well, sent members of the gang here to get checked out before Liz sent them to the pleasure girls in her care. But what about in between those long periods when she was alone out here? Anything could happen. People were getting desperate as the climate continued to grow cold.

A woman living alone would be easy pickings for the gangs of men who were now roving around looking for easy prey, as well as the cannibals who preferred eating humans. Those were just a couple of dangers.

She was a doctor. She would be a valuable asset for someone who wanted to kidnap her and sell her services. It was only a matter of time before something bad happened, and he wanted to be here to make sure it didn't.

Durango didn't say anything, and Landon glanced over to see his friend staring up at the ceiling, his mouth pursed in thought. He could see the wheels grinding in his friend's head. Knew he was most likely thinking of the same scenarios like Landon. A decision would have to be made, and it would have to be made soon.

Chapter Four

Liz always baked when she was nervous. Oh, who was she kidding? She was way past nervous. She was aroused.

Durango always aroused her. Even when he'd told her about his sexual fantasies of sharing her with Landon, he'd aroused her. But she'd been terribly embarrassed, too. She was shy in the bedroom. She couldn't imagine being with any other man, except with Durango. It was why she'd never had sex while he'd been gone.

Okay, so she'd masturbate to fantasies about him. About him sharing her. But that was it. She'd thought that had been enough, until he'd shown up with Landon and the stranger.

In reality she couldn't do what he wanted. Fantasies were safe. Reality was different. In reality she would have to face Landon and Tyrell and Durango. She'd be afraid her and Durango's relationship would become strained. Surely he'd get jealous in allowing other men into her bed? At least that's what she'd secretly assumed in the past. Besides, now they weren't even in a relationship. He had no claims on her, and she had none on him.

She'd been surprised at his admission that none of them had been with pleasure girls. Sparks of jealousy had lashed her while they'd been gone as she'd imagined some other woman getting shared between Durango and Landon. These days, due to the Catastrophe, there were many pleasure girls available. It was one way they made a living. She didn't fault them at all.

Her closest friend and neighbor, Teyla Sutton, was a pleasure girl. Or she had been until she'd fallen in love with a client who'd shared her. Who still shared her with two of his friends. Now Teyla was being shared consistently, and she'd confided to Liz that she loved being double penetrated and triple penetrated. Was even considering maybe having another man enter their relationship.

The foursome had seemed so happy the last time they'd visited her here a couple of weeks ago. Their relationship seemed so caring and strong. But of course, their relationship had to be the exception. A woman would have to *want* to be shared. She would have to be confident her relationship would survive something like that.

Not only that, she'd have to survive the embarrassment of being shared. No, she couldn't embrace such a wicked lifestyle, no matter how much she secretly fantasized that she wanted it.

With a sudden burst of anger, or maybe it was more like frustration at not being a liberated woman like her friend, Teyla, Liz pounded her fist into the bread dough she'd been preparing. Why couldn't life be as simple for her as it was for Teyla? Her friend had no problem opening her heart, and her thighs, for three men.

All Liz had to do was say yes to Durango when he asked again. She frowned and took another angry jab at the puffy dough. If Durango ever did ask again.

She punched the dough harder, pretending it was Durango's sorry ass. He probably wouldn't even bother with her uptightness anymore. He would probably just leave.

She pounded the loaf again. He'd leave and never look back. No man could have such patience going without sex for so long.

She smacked the dough again. He would take up with the pleasure girls, and then her heart would be broken all over again.

Even thinking that, she knew it wasn't true. Durango loved her. He'd come back to her, and she trusted him when he said he and Landon and even the stranger hadn't been with other women. She trusted that he wanted just her. That they wanted just her.

Any woman would be envious that three men wanted her sexually. Wouldn't they? Secretly, she was excited and aroused. Wished she could be more bold and adventurous and just jump in with both feet and do what she wanted. Be with three men.

She gave the pliant dough another smack.

"I can think of a better way to work out other than pounding bread." Durango's friend, Landon, chuckled from the direction of the hall that led to the kitchen. Her head snapped up, and she found him standing there, wearing nothing but low-slung jeans and some mighty nice dark-tanned muscles lacing his fit body. Her heart did this wonderful flip as he grinned sexily at her.

His gaze captured hers. Held hers. She swallowed at his insinuation. Knew he was talking about pounding his cock into her. That thought had the erotic heat flushing through her, but it was quickly forgotten when he winced after taking a step forward onto his injured leg. He weaved dangerously.

Damn his stubborn hide. Hadn't she instructed him to stay in bed? Come to think of it, she couldn't remember saying that, but surely he was smart enough to know he shouldn't be hobbling around on an injured leg. What was it with men? Why were they so stubborn?

Irritation turned to concern as she forgot the dough and rushed to his side before he fell over onto his face. Wrapping her arm around his waist, she tried hard to ignore the bunch of hard muscles flexing against her flesh as she led him into the kitchen. He slumped heavily into a chair.

Muscles on a man, any man, always turned her on. Looking at them. Touching them. Kissing them. The sight of them, the taste and the texture, made her hot.

Durango had always joked about that with her. Said she had a muscle fetish. And now with these three heavily muscled men in her home…sleeping in her bed…Liz blew out a tense breath and quickly moved away from Landon, who she noticed smelled very nice. A tinge of tobacco mingled with scents of wood smoke and his own unique musky smell. A complementary odor to say the least.

"You do that a lot," he muttered.

"What?"

"Run away from your feelings."

"Excuse me?" What in the world was he talking about?

"The way you just reacted when you held me. It wasn't lost on me."

Asshole. Her face flamed. "You're delusional."

"You're in denial."

Oh my God. First Durango and now Landon. She had a mind to kick him out of her kitchen. Better yet, out of her home!

"I've been wanting you for a long time, Brandy."

Lovely. She didn't reply as she began kneading her bread again. She did, however, wonder exactly how long he'd wanted her.

"He talks about you."

Durango talked about her? Great. He probably told them stories of how uptight she was with his kinky sharing fetish.

"Usually when we've been on the trail for a long time, he pulls out your picture and passes it around the camp for all the guys to see."

Son of a bitch. He couldn't share her, so he shared her picture? She wondered what he said about her. Did he tell them about their bedroom romps? Brag about how many times he could make her come in one night?

"He says your whimpers are sexy as sin." His voice had turned low. Soft. Gentle. Seductive.

She should stop him from speaking this way about her.

"He especially likes it when you make those cute mewling sounds when he sucks on your nipples."

Oh, have mercy. It was getting too warm in here.

"Are you trying to seduce my woman already, Landon? I told you I wanted to watch." Lust etched Durango's deep voice as he strolled into the kitchen.

She should have been relieved that Durango had interrupted. She wasn't. She was properly pissed off. Any man who was seriously interested in a woman wouldn't allow another man to speak like this to her while he listened in. He shouldn't be sharing intimate details about her either. How humiliating.

"Hey, Doc," he whispered.

He wrapped his arms around her waist and pressed his chest into her back, pushing his enormous erection against her ass. At the same time he nuzzled the left side of her neck, just like he'd never been away at all. Like no one was watching.

"Durango...Ethan..." She wanted to tell him to stop, but she couldn't quite say the words. She...um...liked what Durango was doing. Liked that another man was watching them. Landon's gaze held hers.

She swore his eyes grew darker. Predatory. The pink tip of his tongue peeked out, and his eyelids drooped to half-mast. He looked very interested in what Durango was doing to her, and Liz felt the simmering need for sex shift beneath her tight control.

"I've missed you, Doc," he whispered against her neck.

I can feel how much, she answered silently, and despite not wanting to, she melted against his strong body. She knew she should mount a protest at doing this in front of Landon, but the stranger held her gaze. The sultry way Durango moved against her made her feel utterly helpless to do anything but feel.

Boy was she ever feeling. His hands were sliding over her hips like two hot brands of wicked intention. She shivered as sultry sensations caressed her flesh, and she found herself both responding and resisting.

"Durango...I can't...shouldn't..." She could barely keep her eyes open as Landon kept watching them. She felt intoxicated with Durango's wild scent as it curled around her in erotic waves.

"I want to make love to you, Doc. Here. Now. Right in front of Landon." Durango's voice sounded tense, and savage. As savage as the way Landon was watching them.

Shock literally shook her. Was Durango crazy? She shouldn't do this. Not in front of someone. She couldn't...*oh my*...Landon was standing. He shouldn't be standing on his injured thigh, her doctor side warned. But the warning was quickly forgotten. Her eyes widened and her pussy creamed as Landon's tanned muscles in his arms jumped and bunched when his hands went to undo the clasp at his jeans. He held her gaze as he peeled down the zipper.

Oh goodness, they were seducing her. Her mouth went dry as he pulled his jeans past his hips. His underwear quickly followed.

"Don't be afraid of what you need," Durango whispered in her ear. "Of what we both need."

He kissed her neck, that tender area right there where her shoulder and neck met. Oh, such a delicious feeling.

"The old days are gone, babe. We need to live every day now. Need to experience our fantasies today. Never put off until tomorrow." Meaning in these dangerous times, chances were high tomorrow may never come, especially in Durango and his friends' line of work.

She could feel Durango tense against her as Landon's cock uncurled, emerging like a giant purple-flushed serpent. Growing, thickening, swelling to such an enormous length Liz was sure she'd never seen a bigger cock, and in her line of work she'd seen plenty of them. She was employed by several pleasure workers, and she made sure the women as well as the men they serviced were disease free, so she didn't hold back on the intimate exams.

"You are going to enjoy Landon, Doc. Hell, I can tell from the way you've tensed and from the way your breaths are coming faster and harder that you're getting really hot."

Hot was an understatement. She felt as if she were on fire. Obviously Durango knew her better than she did herself.

"Come on, babe," Durango prodded. "Let's live those sexual fantasies we both have. Let's make them real."

Her pussy clenched as she watched Landon hobble back to the chair where he sat down. He grasped his big cock with both hands and began to stroke himself.

Liz's fingers suddenly ached to touch him. She didn't dare move to do so.

She froze as Durango's hands came around her waist, and he pulled the sash on her dress to allow it to fall open. Then, from behind her, he unzipped the dress all the way down the front, obviously giving Landon a glimpse of her breasts.

Her breathing quickened even more as Landon kept watching them. Her gaze remained glued to the sensual way he caressed his cock with slow, deliberate, controlled strokes. She barely felt her dress whisper over her shoulders as Durango removed it from her. He dropped it to the ground, and Liz creamed as Landon's gaze darkened with appreciation as he studied her breasts.

She tensed even more as Durango's fingers slipped beneath the waistband of her leggings, catching her undies as well.

"You won't need any clothes covering you anymore, Liz. You have three men to do that."

Oh God.

As he peeled the leggings and panties down, cool air brushed against her thighs and her legs.

She trembled and her lower belly clenched in anticipation as she stepped out of the clothes and stood in front of both of them clad in only her socks. Landon's predatory look intoxicated her and made her breathless.

"You are one beautiful woman, Elizabeth," Landon said. His voice sounded tight. Very aroused. Unbelievably aroused.

"Very beautiful," Durango whispered, and she gasped as he cupped her breasts in his big palms, his fingers erotically grazing her nipples.

She held back another moan as Durango nuzzled his bristly chin against her left shoulder. He continued to tweak and caress her nipples until they were ultrasensitive. They throbbed with his every brush, and her pussy pulsed as she watched Landon continue to stroke his cock. She saw the lust motor through him as his eyelids were lowering, but he was still watching and enjoying the erotic scenery.

"I've wanted to do this for so long, Doc. Knowing that you were dreaming this every night while I was gone."

The seductive tone of his voice was reeling her into his naughty world. She could feel herself melting against his hard body, her own body humming as he ground his thick erection against her buttocks.

"We're going to need to put a plug in you, babe. It's been so long since I've been there. And I don't want you to be hurt when Landon and Tyrell take you there when they get their strength back. They're fast healers, so it won't be long."

Liz couldn't believe how easily he spoke about sharing her. She couldn't believe how aroused she'd become either. She actually *wanted* Durango to take her here right in front of Landon.

Durango let go of her breasts, letting his hands slide down her sides, his fingers trailing over her skin like little bursts of fire. His touch disappeared as he instructed her to do something she'd never done before.

"I want you to walk over to Landon. Position yourself in front of him. Spread your legs, babe, and bend over and take him into your mouth."

Oh sweet mercy, was she hearing right?

He continued with his instructions. "Hold your ankles with your hands while I put the plug in you and then I'll take you from behind."

She couldn't believe he was asking her to do this. Couldn't believe how much she was creaming. She swore her thighs were literally drenched from her arousal.

She nodded jerkily and walked toward Landon. His eyes were laced with desire as he watched her every move. Her legs trembled as he stared up at her. Lust strained his face, and his hands stroked his cock harder.

"Elizabeth. Brandy," he whispered. Unmistakable need was etched in his voice. She felt the need powering through her, too.

Liz licked her lips, shuddered, not from revulsion, but from a sense of euphoria and freedom.

She'd only taken Durango into her mouth. No one else. Now he was asking her to go down on his friend.

"That's it, baby. Now spread your legs," Durango instructed.

She did as Durango said, growing hotter at his dark command. An aroused whimper escaped her lips as she bent over, her face perching over Landon's lap.

Landon held his cock steady with his hands, and she quickly covered the mushroom-shaped cockhead, taking his stiff, pulsing flesh into her mouth. Landon swore, and his cock violently jerked against her tongue.

She moved her head downward, allowing more of his flesh inside. He stretched her lips, and she grabbed her ankles, held them tight, knowing that Durango loved his sex rough and fast. So did she.

She yelped around Landon's cock as Durango caressed her ass cheeks with his hands. He touched her lovingly, slowly, erotically, and she struggled to keep her mind on the task at hand. Going down on Landon.

She tensed as one hand slipped off her buttocks and slid between her soaked thighs. He cursed softly as his fingers touched her wetness.

"She's really liking this, Landon. I told you I know her better than she knows herself."

"She's good. Damned good." Landon hissed between his teeth, his eyes tightly closed as pleasure streamed across his face.

She couldn't help but smile at their conversation. She sucked harder, heard Landon inhale sharply. Yes, he liked what she was doing. He liked it a lot.

Durango's breaths were getting louder and raspier. She heard the slurp of lubricating jelly and imagined him placing a liberal amount over her biggest plug. Suddenly the plug was pressing against her sphincter. The lube was cool, the pressure hot as he stretched her anus and pushed deeper inside.

"You'll wear this always, removing it when you need to clean it, and then you'll put it back in. When we take you, it'll be without warning. We will take you whenever we want. Any one of us. One-on-one or in a group. Understood?"

She nodded, creamed, her senses exploding. She simply could not believe what Durango was saying or how excited it made her feel to think any one of them could take her whenever they wanted. "When Tyrell gets better, and I'm pretty sure it will be sooner rather than later, he'll be wanting you, too. Bad. Keep sucking on Landon."

Liz blinked at the last sentence and realized she'd stopped doing Landon in her fascination from listening to Durango. She knew she should mount a protest. Knew she should fight this carnal excitement, but all she could do was moan around Landon's cock as the thickest part of the plug passed her tender opening and the pressure increased.

Landon moaned. The sound was wonderfully erotic as she began bobbing her head over his erection in quick motions. His thick flesh stretched her lips unbelievably, and the plug expanded her anus as its largeness finally lodged.

"Done," Durango whispered, and she hissed as he caressed her ass cheeks lovingly. "I've waited so long for this. Waited to take you this way."

The rip of foil followed. A condom. She heard the whisper of Durango's jeans lowering. Eagerness rocked her and she swore every sense of hers came alive, making her intricately aware of the man behind her and the man she was sucking. Her legs were trembling with anticipation as she waited for Durango's touch.

Instead, Landon grabbed her attention. His hands thrust into her hair, his fingers tangling and holding onto her strands. Erotic pain seared through her scalp, making her intensely aware of what was happening to her body. The violent awareness, the heat deep inside her vagina, the insistent clenching of her ass as it greedily grabbed the butt plug.

Durango was right, she admitted to herself. He was right about her. She did want more than one man in her sex life, but only as long as Durango remained in the picture.

She took more of Landon's rigid cock into her mouth. His flesh was solid and swollen, and she bobbed her head to slide him in and out several times before bringing him fully out again.

Pain lashed her scalp again as Landon's grip tightened, indicating he wanted her to continue what she was doing. She realized she loved the pain screaming through her scalp. Wanted more of it.

She worked her tongue beneath his cock, stroking his flesh, and then sucked only his pulsing cockhead into her mouth this time. Her tongue lashed his slit, and she grazed her teeth lovingly along the smooth flesh. He liked it, for his grip on her hair became stronger, unleashing another burst of pain in her scalp. The splash of pain seemed like euphoria, and she trembled at its intensity.

Between her thighs, Durango stroked her clit. He pinched and rubbed and massaged with a roughness she loved. Within seconds the carnal convulsions of climax snapped through her, and that was when Durango entered her. His cock thrust into her so hard and so hot and in one quick, solid plunge, impaling her to the hilt, tossing Liz into a wall of arousal that swallowed her whole. Gyrating her hips, she jerked her mouth around Landon's cock as Durango withdrew and powered into her again.

Vibrations rocked her, and she fought to keep sucking Landon. The sensations were a whiplash of pleasure, violent and awesome at the same time. Durango pumped into her harder and harder, throwing her into one orgasm after another. As she drifted into the ecstasy, she heard Landon cursing softly. Could feel his cock pulsing and jerking, his hips trembling as he held himself from coming. Then finally, he cut loose, his guttural groans slashing into the air and meeting Durango's strangled shout as both men came at the same time.

Chapter Five

Oh man, he should have stayed in bed and kept trying to sleep, Tyrell thought as he reluctantly moved back down the hallway, slipping into the bedroom. Quietly, he closed the door, and padded toward the bed. Kicking off his shoes and socks, he removed his jacket, shirt, and jeans, and then slipped back under the covers of the king-sized bed.

Elizabeth's sexy scent drifted up from the pillow and the sheets. Flowery, delicate, and dainty. Just like her. Her smell was what had kept him from falling into a deep sleep.

Earlier, he'd awoken, and was unable to fall back into slumber land due to her scent and the discomfort in his wounded side, compliments of that damned bullet.

It was a bullet he hadn't been able to dodge once the bank guard started shooting during the robbery in progress he and the rest of the Durango Gang had been involved in. Crap, there had been five members of the Durango Gang inside the bank. Obviously one of them had missed a weapon during the weapons search. Well, hell, they'd managed to subdue the son of a bitch anyways, but not until three of them had been shot.

Their leader, Kayne, always drilled it into them that he didn't want anyone hurt. That they must have cool heads at all times and not retaliate to the point of killing someone. Tyrell and the other guys had always maintained that command, and for his troubles he'd taken a couple of bullets during his few months with the gang.

It still pissed him off that rumors were circulating that members of the Durango Gang were murderers, even when they hadn't killed anyone. There was nothing he could do about that though. But the rumors of Durango's lady, Liz, were true. The guys who'd met her said she was a beauty, and Tyrell had now seen it first hand.

She was almost as tall as the three of them. Had a nicely tanned, curvy body, her skin looking so velvety smooth all over. Hard not to miss her body when he'd heard the groans and her whimpers erupting from the kitchen area earlier. Like any curious red-blooded male he'd of course come in to take a look, and man, the lust had slammed into his gut like a sucker punch, sledgehammer, and two-by-four, all at once. His body had tightened into awareness mode, and his cock had snapped into rigid-pole alert mode within a second. Boy had *that* hurt, in a good way of course.

Despite arriving on the tail-end of things, he'd caught sight of her well-developed biceps, a pair of nice slender legs, and a faint dusting of freckles across her shoulders, but that view had been blocked as Durango had moved in between him and her while he'd prepared her with a butt plug.

Oh yeah, he was going to enjoy taking this woman. Enjoy bringing her fantasies to life, as well as bringing Durango's to life as well.

It seemed to take an eternity before Durango and Landon crawled into bed on either side of him. They smelled of sex and *her*. Of course that hadn't helped his fiercely throbbing cock and swollen balls. When he finally did fall asleep, he dreamed about Elizabeth, a woman who would be shared by three men. That is, if she allowed it to happen.

* * * *

"Why are you acting so weird?" Liz's friend, Teyla Sutton, smiled over the cup of coffee Liz handed her before sitting down on the chair across from her at the kitchen table.

Liz tried hard not to grimace as the butt plug zipped a wee bit deeper when she sat. She also tried hard not to think about what had happened earlier today right here in the kitchen. The chair where Landon had sat was empty now, both men satisfied and wanting to help Liz get cleaned up, but she'd insisted they head back into the bedroom to rest because they would only be underfoot.

The strange thing was she hadn't been the least embarrassed after the sex with the two of them. She'd wanted more, but she'd needed to gather her composure and her thoughts about what had happened. She needed to figure out why it had happened and why she'd submitted so easily to Durango's commands, especially since she'd been telling herself all these months that she would be strong and not give in to her fantasies or submit to Durango.

After the sex, Liz had contemplated going back down to the river for yet another bath in the cold water to soothe her aching pussy, but remembered how the water lapping against her pussy had made her feel so wickedly aroused the last time she'd been there. She knew she wasn't aching due to the awesomely powerful thrusts of Durango's cock but because she longed to have him pistoning into her again.

Instead of going to the creek she'd done a quick sponge bath in the living room. Thankfully, she hadn't been interrupted until about an hour later. Liz had just put on some coffee to figure out what in the world she was going to do next with the three men when Teyla had come knocking at her door.

She said she'd been dropping in for a visit while her three men worked in a nearby pasture, cutting hay for the horses, using some old-fashioned hand sickles they'd found in an abandoned barn on the far side of the valley.

"Liz? Did you hear me? How come you're acting so weird?"

Teyla said that Liz was acting weird? Well, hell yeah, she did just have sex with two guys. She was wired and ready to go at it again. She felt like she was in heat or something. Deliciously out of control.

Liz plastered on a fake smile for her suspicious friend. "Weird? I am? Oh, um, I'm just sleepy. The thunderstorm kept me awake," she lied.

Teyla frowned with puzzlement, her eyes sharpening as she studied Liz. "I thought there were just a couple of low rumbles."

Oh great. She'd been up at the crack of dawn, too?

"Would you like some sugar with your coffee?" Liz said, trying to change the subject. She reached for the sugar jar she kept in the middle of the table and noticed her hands were trembling.

Oh darn.

Teyla's gaze narrowed as she also caught sight of Liz's shaking hands. "They're here, aren't they?"

"Excuse me?" Liz's face flamed, giving her away.

Teyla's mouth dropped open. "And you've had sex with them already, haven't you? That's why you're acting so weird."

"Keep your voice down," Liz whispered, not wanting to wake up the men. At least not yet.

"With all three of them? I thought you said you weren't going to give in to Durango if he ever came back?"

Shock mingled with glitters of amusement and excitement in her friend's eyes.

"How did you know there were three? And how do you know he's back?"

Teyla shrugged her shoulders. "They dropped by yesterday afternoon. They looked pretty beat. I wanted to help fix their wounds, but all three refused. Durango said he would wait until you patched them all up."

All three? What?

"Durango was wounded, too?" She hadn't seen any other injuries on him. Just the one in his arm. The one he said she'd put there. Or had she? Why would Durango make her feel so guilty if she wasn't responsible? Anger flared, and Liz swore softly beneath her breath. So she would allow him to keep them here, that's why he'd lied.

"Gosh, you really are rattled. You can't even remember the wound to his arm?"

Liz shook her head, totally pissed at being duped.

Grabbing her coffee mug, she took a tentative sip of the scalding black bitter liquid and felt the heat zip down her throat. It reminded her of having Landon's hot, pulsing cock in her mouth. Oh great, she was already addicted to sex with two men.

Suddenly Teyla squirmed with excitement in her seat and clasped her hands together with overly obvious delight. "Okay, you are really blushing now, Liz. What did they do to you?"

Liz closed her eyes and shook her head, feeling really embarrassed now. She didn't make it a habit of talking about sex. She spoke to her clients about *their* sexual escapades, but she tended to keep her affairs a secret. Okay, affairs might not be the right word. Sharing wouldn't be considered an affair if Durango was in on it and wanted it, right?

"I couldn't refuse them. It was Durango and Landon. I thought I could, but they're just so…"

"Sexy?" Teyla prodded.

Yeah, there was that. "Insistent," Liz said.

"Hot?"

Liz nodded. "And so demanding. Durango put a plug in me."

"Oh my gosh," Teyla breathed and threw up her hands over her mouth, obviously excited that she'd spoken too loud.

"And he said they would take me whenever *they* wanted," Liz confessed, remembering Durango's dark, erotic words.

"You must have made him really hot if he's assuming you're going to go for that. What did you tell him? Did you set him straight? Tell him that they would take you whenever *you* wanted to?"

"No, I just…accepted it. The firm way he spoke made me even more aroused." Was she a sick woman or what?

"Oh wow, this is awesome. I'm so excited for you. To have three men just taking you whenever…well, actually, that's what my three men do, but you were supposed to be different. Stronger than me. Defiant. Professional doctor. Girl power and all that."

Liz could see the sides of Teyla's lips struggling to lift and realized her friend was kidding her.

"I want to experience more of it," Liz confessed, totally not believing she was confessing this out loud and to Teyla.

"That's good to hear."

Liz forgot to breathe as Durango's low voice rumbled over her like smooth black velvet.

"Hi, Ethan." Teyla waved to an area behind Liz and then winked at Liz.

Panic snapped through her. Oh God. Durango was up already and he'd heard her confession? Oh sweet heavens. This was so not good. What about Landon? And the other one? Had they heard, too? Were they standing behind her as well? She dared not look.

Oh, she was so not ready to deal with them. Not now. Not when she had Teyla sitting here, her eyebrows raised with curiosity, obviously awaiting Liz's next move.

"Hey, doll. Nice to see you. I thought I heard voices. Your guys around, Teyla?"

"They're over in the west field. There's some good grass for hay there," Teyla answered, taking a nonchalant sip of her coffee, acting totally normal and pretending that what Liz had just told her didn't affect her one way or the other.

Liz could feel him all around her, and the tension zipping from him to her screamed sex. When he walked into her view, her insides melted. He wore nothing but his hip-hugging blue jeans and those perfectly sculpted, tanned muscles...Liz swore she was hot flashing just looking at them, although she was nowhere near menopause.

"I see Liz took care of that bullet wound for you."

Liz saw Durango stiffen, and obviously he knew the cat was out of the bag. He didn't answer. He also averted Liz's gaze.

Son of a bitch. She would deal with him the moment Teyla was gone. He could bet on that.

"I think I'll get dressed and pop on over and give your guys a hand, Tey. I'll go out the back way. Nice seeing you again."

"Likewise, Ethan," Teyla chirped. A bit too happily where Liz was concerned. But then again, Teyla was always happy these days with three men sexually satisfying her, protecting her, and loving her.

They both waited for Durango to disappear down the hallway before Teyla leaned over the table and whispered softly, "He is so hunky. And the other two are, too. My goodness, Dr. Liz, you certainly do have the hottest male patients, and I'm not only speaking of your guys, but the last three guys you sent my way," Teyla gushed.

Then her mouth dropped into a quick frown. "I wonder sometimes what would have happened to me if Logan, Cass, and Spencer hadn't arrived when they did. I love them all so dearly. I dread anything happening to them, especially if those vigilantes decide they want to go after them for their part in the Durango Gang. Has Ethan said anything to you about quitting?"

That last question hit Liz in the gut like a bullet, and she sucked in a sharp breath at the impact. With all this sexual tension between her and Durango, she hadn't really thought about it. Yet, here it was, poised over her head like a guillotine.

Teyla's brows furrowed with concern. "You have talked to him about this. I mean, you can't just allow them to have sex with you and then just leave. That's just not right, Liz. You deserve better. You have to demand better for yourself. When he leaves, it will hurt you just like the last time. Maybe you don't remember, but I do. You were a basket case for weeks."

"I can handle this. I will handle this. I want this. I *need* this."

"Be practical, Liz. You don't need to be a pleasure girl for them."

"But you were one." Those words escaped her mouth, and from the pained expression on Teyla's face, Liz knew she shouldn't have said anything. Besides being a friend, Teyla was also her client. She needed to remember to remain sensitive.

"It was different for me. I needed the money."

I need the sex. Masturbation was good and all, but she needed the sex with Durango and the others. Had been craving it like a drug ever since Durango had brought up the subject months ago before he'd left. Before even meeting him, she'd dreamt of having ménages with strangers, but she'd been too damned shy to follow through on anything.

Oh man, she must be twisted or something. No, actually, that wasn't true. Durango wasn't twisted, and he wanted the same as her.

"I can handle this," Liz replied with renewed firmness.

"You love him, so I bet you can." Teyla smiled, and Liz felt confidence burn through her.

Yes, I can. She just hoped she wasn't deluding herself.

* * * *

Ethan Durango found Logan Leigh working an iron pole as he tried prying a giant boulder from the clutches of the hard field. In the distance, Spencer and Cassidy led a couple of black horses that dragged a funny-looking contraption that seemed to mow down the tall, yellowing grass, spreading it over the land.

Ethan couldn't help but grin. It looked like a sight right out of a pioneer movie. Old-fashioned harvesting with horses. Despite the icy bite of the wind blowing against them, he noticed perspiration drenching Logan's shirt and his forehead. His hands looked red and cold as he gripped the metal pole and pushed this way and that way trying to dislodge the boulder.

Logan and the other guys worked so unwaveringly that, to Ethan's disappointment and concern, none of the men took the time to look around to see if a lynching party was coming for them. Had the trio of ex-gang members relaxed so much they'd let down their guard?

Man, this farmer stuff just wasn't like the men he'd come to know in the gang. As far as he knew the closest any of them had come to farm work was tilling the soil with a rototiller in their backyards. Teyla sure had changed them from alert men to relaxed farmers.

Amazing.

Ethan wasn't sure if he could feel so relaxed if he was put into this same position. Running with the Durango Gang had made him alert, lean, and hungry for violence against the men and women who were taking advantage of the regular people in need. Yeah, sure, he could go into politics and run for office and change things that way.

Unfortunately there was no government to run for. People were fending for themselves since the Catastrophe. There were no social safety nets in place, no health care, and food was certainly lacking. The only thing that spoke these days was money, and that was where he came in by taking from the rich and giving to the poor. Not that he literally gave to the poor. He gave the money to soup kitchens that were opening up in the cities. He'd even helped dish out the food he'd bought and brought to these places.

His stealing was what made him a criminal, and he now appeared on most wanted posters pretty much everywhere. Truth was, he felt like he was making a difference, and to him that's what counted. It beat feeling useless and fending for himself. The only problem was every time he sent money back with one of the guys who dropped in to check on Liz, she'd refused it.

Her refusal pissed him off, but he understood her principles and why she preferred to live the way she did, accepting whatever a client could give her for her services. She was a giver. Not a taker.

It had always impressed him that she was so giving. That was one of the reasons he'd fallen in love with her. Another reason, of course, was her pretty face and her concern for him when he'd sliced his palm open on that hot, humid day in the garage.

"Backbreaking work, is it?" Durango asked from where he stood watching.

Before Durango could blink Logan had palmed a gun from out of nowhere and pointed it right at Ethan's chest.

Ethan swallowed as fear cleaved into him. Instantly he realized his mistake. The scenery had looked serene, but Logan appeared to have known he was here the whole time. Shit. The guy certainly hadn't lost his touch, had he?

"Shouldn't sneak up on a man like that, Ethan. You know better than that. Had you been anyone else we would have taken you down the minute you entered the field." Logan chuckled and nodded to his right.

Realizing he'd forgotten to breathe, Ethan inhaled deeply and followed Logan's gaze to where Cassidy and Spencer now stood not more than thirty feet away, their guns drawn, aiming at Ethan. Their faces were stern and tight. Obviously he should have announced his arrival. He wouldn't be coming in quietly where these guys were concerned. At least, not anymore.

"Easy, boys. I come in peace," Ethan said as he slowly lifted his hands in a submissive motion. "What's gotten up your asses?"

Suddenly all three men started laughing and Ethan relaxed. The bastards were toying with him. He hoped.

In seconds, the men had surrounded Ethan and were back-slapping him and returning to their own jovial, if not uptight selves.

"Daylight is burning, my man. Have you come to lend us a hand?" Logan asked as Cassidy and Spencer quickly said their good-byes and headed back to their horses.

Logan's grin sobered, yet his eyes glittered with mischievous amusement. "Shit, forgot you had an arm injury. Better not help, or Dr. Liz will be giving us shit for taking you out of action. You need both arms to hug that babe."

"The wound isn't that bad," Ethan said as he pulled his collar up around his neck trying to ward off the cold wind. "I have one free hand. Let me put it to good use."

"Grab a hold and start pushing down. We'll get this fucking boulder rolled out of the way yet."

Ethan clutched near the top of the icy bar, and Logan clasped beneath his hand. The men started pushing down, and to Ethan's surprise he saw the boulder begin to budge.

"Keep pushing," Ethan instructed and bore down. In a couple of minutes they had the boulder out of the dirt and rolled off to the side of the field.

"Thanks, you came in really handy." Logan chuckled, and they began to walk along the field looking for more boulders to dig up and get out of the way.

"I guess you're putting down roots here since you're clearing the fields."

Logan nodded, a huge smile plastered on his face. "Yeah, we're staking our claim around these parts. We figure clearing the rocks now will help us move the sickle-bar mower faster. We don't want downtime due to repairs. Those rocks are hidden behind the tall grass, and if the guys know the land is clear then we can get more work done in a day."

"That's a good idea," Durango acknowledged as he kept up the fast walking pace with Logan, who kept to a straight line and his gaze glued to the tall grass in front of him.

"Heard that the vigilantes weren't too happy with your latest heist," Logan said after a few moments of silence. "I'd watch your back while you're here. I think you might even make sure that you get Liz armed to the tooth if you plan on leaving her alone again. They may come seeking revenge on you through her, even though they believe you two have split."

A bad feeling slithered through Ethan at Logan's warning. Fear for her safety was something Ethan had to deal with on a regular basis. When he sent guys from the gang to bring her money, he also sent letters telling her it wasn't safe where she was. She always sent back word that she was quite capable of taking care of herself.

"You might also want to consider getting out of the gang. Remember what happened to your cousin Kayne's girlfriend?" Logan said.

Another wave of cold fear sliced through him at the mention of Eve. Kayne and some of the gang had taken a shine to a pleasure girl working out of a pleasure house over in a British Columbia town on the other side of the Rocky Mountains. The vigilantes had found out, kidnapped her, and taken her deep into the mountains to some hideaway retreat. No one knew what had happened to her there, but somehow, she'd escaped. She'd refused to see Kayne and the gang again.

Ethan couldn't let something bad happen to Doc. He'd been selfish in coming back without a plan. He realized that now. His lust for Doc had made him brainless. His desire for adventure had put her life in danger, and deserting her the way he had was really stupid on his part.

"Not only because of what happened to Eve, but because after you left yesterday evening we had company."

Ethan stiffened. "Posse? We covered our tracks."

"No, an elderly neighbor who was in town the other day dropped by to say she heard rumors about roving cannibal-type gangs starting to move from cities into secluded areas where it's easier to subdue their victims. They torture victims until the person or persons tell the whereabouts of nearest surviving friends or family. When these cannibals are full, they kill their half-eaten victims and move onto these houses the tortured ones have told them about. They catch their prey and stay until the food, so to speak, runs out. We were going to drop by later to pick up Teyla and pass along the information."

Jesus. Logan was a bounty of good news today, wasn't he?

"Any ideas how close these cannibals are?" Ethan asked as he found himself looking for hidden boulders as well.

"Still far off. Other side of the mountains. I'm sure they'll be in the area soon. Maybe if our luck holds out they'll stay away until after the winter. That is, if the winter ends this time around."

Logan swallowed back a curse. He'd felt the weather getting colder every year. The Catastrophe had really screwed the climate. He should really consider taking Liz south of the border, but down that way it truly wasn't any better. It was cold everywhere. He was surprised grass kept growing, although it was starting to look twisted and unhealthy.

They worked quietly after that, each lost in their own thoughts as they searched and dug out the boulders. It wasn't long before Ethan wished for a nice warm pair of gloves. His hands were so fucking cold.

But he figured if Logan could handle the cold, so could he. As he worked he kept thinking about Liz and how he could protect her without driving himself crazy with the feelings of uselessness that had plagued him up until he'd joined the Durango Gang. There, in the gang, he felt as if he was doing some good. Unfortunately, he'd missed Liz from the moment he left, until he'd come home and found her safe. Had it only been earlier this morning?

He'd already taken her twice. Once orally, once vaginally while she went down on Landon. Was he some sort of sex-crazed maniac? Using her and then throwing her away when he wanted to head off for an adventure again?

That would make him a really selfish son of a bitch. Undeserving of Liz. She was too good for him. He should have realized that a long time ago. Yet, he couldn't let her go because she was the best thing in his life. That thought sobered him. If she was the best thing in his life, then why in hell was he treating her the way he'd been since leaving?

Chapter Six

The house was quiet. Too quiet, Ethan thought as he stood on the other side of the river watching the thick white spirals of fog block out the surrounding jagged mountains in the distance and settle over the valley, caressing the century-old stone house. Hell, it was even quieter than when they'd arrived in the rain early this morning.

Teyla had shown up an hour ago where they'd been working, telling Logan that it was time for them to go back home, meaning their place. She'd been acting easygoing as if nothing was wrong back here, which meant if something had happened it had happened within the past hour.

The cozy way Teyla had nestled against Logan and the sultry way she was eyeing Cassidy and Spencer as they walked quickly to greet her made Ethan realize the three men would be giving her some hot, tender loving tonight. Suddenly he hadn't been able to wait to get back home himself.

Home. The word made him feel all warm and bubbly inside. Made his heart happy. Yet the moment he'd realized no spiral of smoke wafted from the fireplaces and no buttery glow of lights drifted from the windows of the house in the gloomy twilight, alarm bells began to go off inside his head.

Maybe what Logan had said earlier about the cannibals coming meant they were already here? He couldn't see the lean-to where they'd stabled the horses from here, but even if they were there, it didn't mean anything.

Had the cannibals taken out Landon and Tyrell? The men couldn't get too far with their injuries if their stitches bust open, and riding horses would make their injuries worse.

Liz was a lousy shot even if she tried to shoot straight. Which she didn't, because she refused to take any shooting lessons from him or anyone. Every time he'd brought up the subject of learning to shoot properly she would quote the Hippocratic Oath saying she'd sworn to save lives and not take them.

Fuck. He'd been surprised she'd been using the gun he'd left her when he'd shown up and she'd fired a shot. It had gone wide, but with her carrying a gun, it meant she'd been more scared than she'd been letting on to the guys who'd dropped by to check up on her.

Shit, he'd left her unprotected for months. And today, he'd simply gone off to visit Logan and the guys without a second thought to any security measures. Man, he was a real lousy protector, wasn't he? He resisted the overwhelming urge to start running toward the house.

Okay, he'd already covered the selfish asshole part. Now he was caught out here in the open with anyone inside the house watching his every move. He needed to act as if he didn't suspect a thing. If he went for his gun, then whoever was watching him would know he was on to them. The gun he wore in his holster suddenly felt like a dead, useless weight.

Damn! He would have to keep walking as coolly as possible, acting as if he suspected nothing. His stomach clenched in dread as he neared the house, his gaze sliding off every window pane, looking for the slightest evidence of someone standing to the side watching him. He saw nothing out of the ordinary.

No sound sifted from the house. Just the eerie presence of the cold wind snapping through the branches of the nearby evergreens.

When he neared the front door, he slipped into the evergreens lining the front of the house and held back a groan as fiery pain zipped along his wounded arm. With his fingers feeling numb and icy he could barely hold the gun in his right hand. He switched to his left.

He'd been practicing shooting with his left lately, just in case, yet he'd never been able to accomplish a quick and accurate shot as well as with his right hand. Nothing he could do about that now.

Keeping his back to the tangled ivy climbing up the wall, he quickly turned the corner and edged up to the nearest window. The living room. The curtains weren't drawn, and he peeked inside. Darkness shrouded the furniture. Nothing moved.

Frig! Maybe the cannibals had grabbed Liz, Landon, and Tyrell and taken off with them?

His heart crashed against his chest as he crouched and ducked beneath the window and did the same with another living room window further down. Popping around the corner, he peeked into the next window he came across. A bedroom. No one there.

He came to the back door, held his breath, and twisted the doorknob. It was unlocked. Oh, great. Either the intruders had watched Teyla leave and weren't expecting him or they'd left the back door unlocked because they were making it look like nothing was wrong.

The moment he pushed open the door a crack he smelled it. The scent of baking bread. Totally normal. Yet he hadn't seen any smoke from the oven or the fireplace. Totally not normal.

And then he heard something. A soft whisper. A sultry whimper.

What the fuck?

He resisted the urge to charge in blindly. Held himself in check as he stopped visions of any intruders attacking Liz. Doing to her what had been done to Eve.

Chill, man! Chill. Don't think it.

He forced his breaths to slow. Forced himself not to panic. Stepping into the back hallway, he aimed the gun in front of him, expecting someone to step out of any one of the three bedrooms. Nothing happened.

Except he could now hear grunts. Male grunts that sounded oddly like Landon.

He stopped in front of the closed door of the bedroom he and Liz had once shared. The room the guys and he had taken over. Soft, sexy whimpers drifted to his ears. He could hear the sound of bed springs creaking. Landon moaning. Tyrell groaning.

Damn! Obviously they'd gotten acquainted faster than he'd expected. He should be pissed off that he wasn't included. He wasn't. He was relieved that nothing bad had happened. Quite to the contrary. Something good was happening. Liz was loosening up.

He twisted the doorknob. It creaked open, and he pushed it inward. The next thing he knew a strong hand was yanking the gun out of his hand, and another hand grabbed his wrist and yanked him inside. It happened so quickly he didn't get a chance to react.

A rough push from behind him had him flying onto the bed with one hell of a jolt. He landed on his gut, pain ripping through his already-sore freaking arm. He tried to get up, but someone strong was flipping him over onto his back and then climbing onto his torso. He came face-to-face with a grinning Landon. In the background he saw Tyrell, with a huge smile on his face.

"What the fuck are you doing? You scared the shit out of me," Durango shouted.

He tried to buck Landon off him, but he realized Liz was standing there and she had the cutest playful smile on her face.

"You've been a very bad boy, Durango. Making me believe that I shot you. I should have known better since I am a lousy shot," Liz said softly as she moved to the head of the bed and reached down, grabbing his left wrist. He inhaled at the sultry way her fingers wrapped around his flesh, and she led his arm up over his head. He tried to look up to see what she had in mind, like he didn't already suspect, but Landon's hand cupped Ethan's chin, holding him firmly so he couldn't see.

Landon's green eyes twinkled with obvious amusement. "Let Liz get her payback, my man. I told you the truth would come out. It always does."

"Payback is a bitch, buddy. Now she gets to tie you up and have a little fun with you." Tyrell chuckled as he walked to the other side of the bed and grabbed his wrist, bringing it up in the same way as Liz was doing.

Immediately Ethan relaxed and stopped struggling. All was well. No cannibals. No posse. Things were good. Just a playful bunch of guys and a woman who were pretending to have sex so they could lure him into the bedroom, tie him up, and let Liz get some payback. He could handle this.

Liz's soft, sultry voice whispered through the air. "I have payback planned against you two for going along with him, so consider yourselves not out of the woods yet."

On top of him Landon tensed. Tyrell's eyes widened in surprise, and maybe even a shade of fear?

"Suckers," Durango joked.

"Fuck off, my man," Landon quipped, but suddenly Durango was sensing messages shooting from his friend. He cast a quick glance at Tyrell, who was also looking a bit weird, and Durango was suddenly getting it.

"Okay," Durango replied, understanding what the eye signals from Landon were meaning.

"Now!" Landon shouted.

He jumped off Durango, who in turn quickly reached out with his wounded arm, groaning and wincing as pain sliced through his injury, but he managed to grab Liz around her waist. She squealed in surprise, and Landon was quickly untying Durango while Tyrell was grabbing restraints on his side of the bed. In seconds, Durango had her on her back, with himself nestled on top of her hips and Landon and Tyrell quickly placing the restraints on her wrists.

Anger and excitement lashed at him from her gorgeous sparkling eyes.

"You bastards! Traitors!" she screamed and laughed at the same time.

"Never threaten two men when their friend is about to be restrained." Landon snorted as he and Tyrell moved to the foot of the bed.

Landon grabbed her left leg. She tried to kick at him with her right leg, but Tyrell managed to grab it before too much damage occurred. Both men managed to tie her ankles without too much trouble. A moment later he climbed off Liz, and all three men stood at the base of the king-sized bed, peering down at her.

She looked properly pissed. And so beautiful. Her blonde hair was a sexy mess, her cheeks were flushed the prettiest pink, her breasts were heaving against her wool dress, and her legging-clad legs were nicely spread. There was only one problem. She was fully clothed.

"I will get you guys for this!" she spat and tugged at her restraints. But they didn't budge.

Durango slapped Landon and Tyrell on their backs, congratulating them on a job well done.

Liz stopped struggling and glared back at the three of them. But Durango saw the heated stare lusting across her face. She liked being tied up. Liked that she had no control over what they would do to her.

"Remember what I said, Doc. We'll take you whenever and wherever we want. We want you now. All three of us."

She visibly shivered at his words, and he heard Tyrell and Landon inhale softly. He saw the fear flash in her pretty blue eyes. Fear and excitement. Whether she knew it or not, she was ready.

"And now, gentlemen, onto our next phase of the plan," Durango quipped. Having said that, he ushered Tyrell and Landon out of the bedroom and followed them.

* * * *

"Do you think you can handle it?" Durango asked Tyrell and Landon as the three of them began undressing out in the hallway.

"Fuck, yeah," Landon growled. "I've been ready since the first time I saw her."

Durango grinned and focused his attention on Tyrell. "You?"

Tyrell nodded. Yeah, his side ached like a bitch, but his cock ached more. Ever since he'd laid eyes on the picture of Liz that Durango shared with the gang all those cold lonely nights on the trail, Tyrell had loved her. Hell, he'd fallen in love with a freaking picture.

She was so cute. A nice set of dimples popping out in her cheeks as she'd smiled for the camera. She looked like the girl next door type. Shy, pretty, and sweet, and to him she was the sexiest-looking woman alive. She was a doorway to life before the Catastrophe, because if Durango hadn't found Liz first, he would have asked her to marry him on their first date.

Durango had never bragged to the gang about his sexual intimacies with the gang. He wasn't that kind of a guy. And Tyrell knew if Durango had bragged publically then he would have socked him in the mouth, telling him he should respect his ex-fiancée, because Tyrell was that kind of a guy.

By the time Durango had approached Ty and asked him to be the third guy to bring Liz's fantasies to life, Ty had been more than ready to meet her. When he had met her, she'd been exactly how Durango had expressed her to be.

Concerned, tender, and passionate. In that order. Oh man, was she ever passionate. The eager way she'd taken Landon into her sweet, pouty mouth had just about made him come in his jeans. The erotic way she'd moaned while Durango had smoothed his hands over her silky ass, then put the plug in and then taken her from behind, had set Tyrell on fire.

When he'd heard Durango tell her that any one of them could take her whenever they wanted and wherever they wanted, Ty had waited for her to protest. She hadn't. Hadn't protested, either, when they'd tied her to her bed. He'd expected her to struggle when he'd brought her arm up and lashed the leather restraints around her wrist. She hadn't. She'd been too willing. Then when she'd kicked out at Landon with her leg and he'd grabbed her ankle, he'd handled her loosely. Had she wanted to, she would have been able to break free. She hadn't. Instead a wild, gorgeous fire danced in her eyes.

She wanted to be taken. Wanted to lose herself in something, yet she hadn't figured out she'd wanted to lose her self-control. And he would make her lose it, too.

"Ready, boys?" Durango asked, his voice breathy and aroused. Tyrell didn't have to gaze down and check if the other two were ready. He sensed the pent-up sexual tension zapping the air like lightning bolts all around them. He knew Liz would feel it, too.

"Condoms? Lube?" Durango asked.

"I placed them in her top right drawer beneath her panties when she wasn't looking earlier," Landon acknowledged.

"Sex toys?"

"Snuck them in from the saddle bags while she was kneading her bread," Tyrell answered.

Both men visibly tensed.

"You men sure know how to pleasure a woman." Tyrell chuckled. "And that's all I'm saying."

He grinned as Landon and Durango cursed softly as they understood he'd been watching while Liz had gone down on Landon and Durango had taken her from behind.

"You weren't as bad off as you were playing, were you?" Durango asked, shaking his head in amazement.

"Playing on a woman's sympathy is what gets me some tender loving care," Tyrell joked, although he really had felt bad before Liz had removed the bullet with such tenderness he'd just about died. "And I can tell she likes me. I noticed the way she looks at my muscles, which by the way are bigger than either of yours."

Durango and Landon grinned widely at him.

"Big talk for a big man, eh?" Landon wiggled his eyebrows, dropping his gaze to Tyrell's extremely long, hard, and swollen erection. "So, let's go and see if size truly matters."

Landon and Tyrell made a move toward the bedroom door behind where Liz was lying restrained on the bed.

But Durango's fingers curled over Ty's and Landon's shoulders, stopping them cold.

"If all three of us go in with our huge sizes, she'll get scared. Her sweet, tight pussy and ass are begging to be taken, but let me go in first and get her ready."

Tyrell knew the man was right. Although privately Durango had told Landon and Tyrell about Liz, and Ty had known about her even before meeting her, she really didn't know him and hadn't slept with Landon either. So yeah, she would be frightened having three big guys coming into the room at the same time. The last thing he wanted was to frighten Liz. So, he'd have to be patient.

Beside him Landon agreed. Tyrell put in his acknowledgement and watched a totally nude Durango open the bedroom door.

* * * *

Due to the sudden turn of events of finding herself tied down on her bed instead of Durango being here, Liz could not believe the wicked excitement lashing her senses. Earlier, after Teyla had left, and Liz had come into the bedroom to inspect Landon's and Tyrell's wounds, they'd noticed her agitation almost immediately. Their concern had her feeling she could confide in them. She'd confessed she'd discovered she hadn't been the one who'd shot Durango after all. When she'd asked if they would help her with a payback plan forming in her mind, they'd eagerly agreed.

She'd trusted them, but she totally understood why they'd turned on her. Their fear of her retribution made her realize the guys felt they needed to stick together. United they conquered, divided they fell, was the old saying. Instead of being angry for too long, she'd realized the loyalty between the three men was as thick as thieves, and it made her happy that such a bond existed between them. They had each other's backs, and that was pretty rare for people these days.

Being tied down here on the bed with three men lurking around in the hallway ready to carry out exquisite, naughty stuff exhilarated her, and it made her imagination come up with all sorts of wicked things. She could hear them whispering in the hallway, and when the door creaked inward, Liz tensed. Realizing she was breathing hard and hoarse, she held her breath and watched and waited.

Durango strolled in, and she exhaled in relief. The relief was short-lived as he was totally naked and fully erect, his toned body laced with muscles. Lots of delicious muscles. Very nice.

Her gaze dropped and her eyes widened at his immense size. She realized she'd forgotten over the months how truly big his erection could get when he was aroused. Or how it made his cock swollen and rigid and flushed to an angry red color, not to mention raising a magnificent web of elevated veins interwoven along the engorged length. She swallowed. Her throat felt suddenly dry with excitement and fear. Her senses were in full alert as he strolled confidently to her dresser and slid open the top right drawer where she kept her panties. He dipped his hand inside the open drawer.

Tension sliced through her. What was he up to in there? She didn't remember him having an underwear fetish. She blinked in surprise when he lifted out several packages along with what was unmistakably a black blindfold.

Oh. How had they gotten there?

She wanted to ask him that question, but she was mesmerized now as he placed the packages and blindfold on one side of the dresser and took out other items. Lying them out on top of the dresser, he lifted lids on boxes, and she realized they were several boxes of condoms as well as tubes of lube and a massive pink dildo. *Have mercy,* she hadn't realized such items were still being produced these days with the chaos running rampant around the world.

"Where…where did you get those?" she questioned softly.

"Abandoned sex toy shop in some deserted town we passed through weeks ago. Of course we thought of you, and we all helped ourselves to some sealed packages."

He said nothing else as he arranged everything on the dresser, and then he moved in front of the items, his back to her, blocking her view. She heard him rip open the other packages that he'd laid at the side of the dresser.

She stretched her neck as much as she could, trying to get a view through the dresser mirror at what other items he had there, but she saw nothing. She did however see the wonderful expression of anticipation on his face. Watching his face in the mirror, she noted his cheekbones were flushed and his eyes filled with lust and eagerness.

She trembled with excitement.

As he turned from the dresser, she spied the blindfold in his hand.

"I'm going to be using this on you," he said as he sat on the edge of the bed near her and placed the blindfold on the pillow beside her head. "It'll heighten your senses. Make you more comfortable with three men your first time."

Her tummy hollowed out in a very nice way at the mention of her being pleasured by three men. She shook her head, not wanting her sight to be cut off, but wanting it at the same time. She realized she was teetering on the edge of doing something she'd been raised to believe was improper, but something she truly wanted and craved. This. Durango and two other men fucking her.

Just then she noticed a smear of blood on the white bandage she'd wrapped around his upper arm wound. Her doctor's training snapped aside her arousal.

"You're bleeding. I should check that."

He shook his head, the tips of his lips lifting into a warm smile. "I'm fine. You don't have to worry, Doc. When I'm around you I don't feel physical pain. I feel pleasure and happiness. I feel *you*, sweetness."

Oh my gosh.

"I feel you are ready, Doc. But I want to hear it from you."

Her, ready? A sudden bout of panic snapped through her, but she forced it away. "I don't know. I don't know if I would ever be ready for something like this," she answered truthfully.

But her body was betraying her brain. Her breasts felt swollen, her nipples tense beneath her wool dress, her pussy creaming. Even as she kept her gaze glued to Durango she could seen how hard and fast her breasts were pressing against the restraints of her clothing.

The plug impaling her ass clenched with a wicked pulsing as her muscles spasmed in an unusual eagerness to be penetrated and her drenched pussy ached to be filled. It seemed over the past several months the only one she'd been kidding was herself.

She wanted Durango and Landon, and she wanted this new man Durango had brought here, too. Why would she want a total stranger to be intimate with her? Because, she realized, Durango and Landon trusted Tyrell, and so she trusted him, too. As if Durango knew what she was thinking, he spoke again.

"Then you'll have to trust me, Doc. Trust me to give you what you crave. What we both crave. Can you do that for me?"

She nodded, realizing she didn't even hesitate. His eyes flared even darker, and she trembled at the erotic intensity of his gaze.

"If there's anything you feel uncomfortable with, say the word no and we'll stop."

She nodded again. Sweet heavens! What was she agreeing to?

"Then I hope you'll forgive me for ruining your clothes," he breathed.

She blinked with momentary puzzlement and gasped as he turned swiftly on the bed, repositioning himself, and suddenly placed both his hands on the lapels of her dress. The harsh sound of clothing ripping and buttons popping off onto the floor shot through the air.

Cool air breathed against her exposed breasts. His palms settled over her mounds, and he squeezed them gently. "Remember, Liz. You are always my heart."

"And you mine," she answered back, loving the intoxicating way he stared at her. He inhaled softly at her words, his smile widening. He remained silent as he began massaging both mounds at the same time, his eyes studying her.

"I like the way your eyelids drift halfway closed whenever I touch your breasts," he murmured. "I like how the tip of your tongue peeks out between your lips when you're aroused."

Her tongue did that? She checked and realized that, yes, her lips had slightly parted and the tip of her tongue was settled there. Lust shone brighter in his gaze as he suddenly lowered his head over her chest area. She stared at his lips, mesmerized by their seductive plump curve as they parted and he sucked her left nipple into his hot mouth.

She jerked, loving the warmth of his mouth as his lips tugged her nipple and the wild sensations raced through her breast, arrowing down to the sensitive areas between her thighs.

Her heart pounded as he took her tender bud between his sharp teeth and held tight as his tongue swiped back and forth across her imprisoned nipple. Her heart beat faster, and she couldn't stop the moan of arousal as sweet bites of pleasure-pain lashed her captive flesh.

Naughty sensations twisted through her, and she became achingly aware of her sexual needs and every erotic spasm rippling through her body. Became in tune with Durango's erratic breathing, the intoxicating waves of heat lapping against her flesh where his hip touched hers, and she loved the lashes of anticipation snapping through her like jolts of electricity.

He let her tender nipple go with a pop and lifted his head. "I know what I'm forcing you into isn't the most conventional of relationships, Doc. But it's a desire we both crave. Something we both need. You wouldn't be twisting and writhing in your sleep when you fantasize if what I'm about to give you isn't what you crave."

She didn't protest as Durango slid a gentle hand beneath her head and slipped the blindfold on. She blinked as darkness enveloped her. Immediately her senses snapped to listening mode.

"I'll let Landon and Tyrell undress the rest of you."

She creamed in her panty at that comment and felt the mattress move as he got up. She listened intently for what he would do next.

Chapter Seven

A moment later she heard him in the area of the dresser. Heard things being moved about on the dresser. When a moment later the bedroom door creaked open and she heard the patter of bare feet as Landon and Tyrell entered the room, her heart began an even more frantic pounding. She heard their sharp inhalations of their breaths and could just imagine how she must look splayed out on the bed, her dress ripped down the middle, her breasts heaving and her eyes blindfolded.

Oh God. The thought of them looking at her like this, tied up, vulnerable, and at their total mercy, shot vibrations of unimaginable anticipation roaring through her. She fought to drag air into her heaving lungs and tensed as fingers slipped beneath the waistband of her leggings.

"Don't move, Brandy, I'm going to relieve you of these." It was Landon. His voice sounded hoarse and husky.

She whimpered in answer. Couldn't for the life of her think of anything to say as her mind shut down and her body responded. Warm knuckles nudged against her flesh, and her tummy tightened. And then she heard ripping as Landon literally tore the leggings right down the middle as Durango had done to her dress. A couple of moments more of ripping sounds, and her leggings were completely off. Now she only wore her socks and panty, and she wouldn't even consider the remnants of her wool dress as being on her. Her socks were quickly peeled from her feet, both at the same time.

"She's gorgeous, Durango." Tyrell breathed from beside her. She felt the mattress move, inhaled sharply as a warm hand cupped her right breast. Cried out shamelessly as a hot mouth enveloped her tender nipple.

A stranger had taken her nipple into his mouth. Oh gosh, this was simply unbelievable. With superb tenderness she didn't know a man could possess, Tyrell squeezed her breast, holding it while he sucked her nipple. Hard. He stayed there at her breast, tugging her nipple with his lips, biting gently and massaging her breast.

She creamed and creamed.

Her tummy tensed again as warm fingers dipped beneath the elastic of her underwear. With one violent tug, Landon ripped them right down the middle and peeled the edges aside. She was now totally naked for them.

"Beautiful, Brandy. More beautiful than I ever had imagined," Landon whispered. She held her breath as the bed moved between her spread legs. "I'm going to return the favor that you gave to me earlier, sweetness."

Hot muscles brushed against the insides of her legs as Landon got into position between them. She cried out and trembled as hot air breathed against her pussy.

"I wanted to take you the moment Ethan brought me home," Landon said from between her legs. "Every night I would stand outside and watch the house. I'd watch as the lights went out, and then I imagined you in bed with Ethan. Wondered how you would react when the time came to invite me into your bed. Somehow I just knew this day would come."

His softly spoken words intoxicated her. She knew he wanted her. It had been written in his gaze every time she caught him looking at her when Landon had lived here with them. But she'd been in denial. Hadn't wanted to believe Durango would allow a strange man access to her body.

Liz jerked as a finger nudged into her creaming pussy.

"Nice and wet for us, aren't you, Doc?" Durango said. "Start doing her, Landon. I'm getting really hot watching Tyrell at her breast. I think I'll join him."

She creamed harder, her pussy throbbing and eagerly clenching around Durango's finger as he began to withdraw.

He swore softly. "Your sweet pussy is greedy, baby. All in good time. You'll have us all, in good time."

Fire lashed through her at his comment. Her breaths came faster, harsher. She cried out as Landon's tongue spread her labia and lashed against her aching clit. He lapped her gently, putting a delicious pressure against her sensitive bud. Within seconds he had her writhing and pulling against her restraints.

Landon. The bastard. He was good. So good with his tongue.

She panted and yelped as Durango, it had to be Durango, sat on the other side of her, because she felt the mattress dip beneath his weight. His large hand palmed her left breast, and she moaned softly as his warm breath whispered against her nipple.

"I'm here, Doc. You look so hot having two other men tending to you. Tyrell sucking your breast and Landon lapping at your cunt. Your cheeks are flushed such a beautiful pink color. I've never seen you look so pretty."

"Durango..." She breathed his name like he was a drug. She didn't say anything else, just his name, over and over again. Maybe she spoke in her mind or maybe out loud, she wasn't sure. She wasn't sure of anything but that she really enjoyed what these three men were doing to her.

Durango took her nipple into his hot mouth and began tugging and pulling and caressing her the same way as Tyrell. Feverish heat lashed her as the three men licked and lapped and bit her.

Then Landon's tongue suddenly disappeared, and a moment later she felt something big and smooth nudge at her vaginal opening.

"I've wanted to fuck you with this pretty pink dildo the moment I saw it," Landon breathed.

He didn't give her a moment to catch her breath before he sunk it into her pussy. Pulling it out gently, he sunk the dildo into her again, and she could hear the slurping sound of her wetness zipping through the air. He slid into her again and again, his thrusts faster and harder, her pussy clutching the invader harder and harder.

Every time he withdrew, he made sure to circle the tender nerve endings in and around her clit with generous pressure of a knuckle, before sliding the big dildo into her again.

The men at her breasts kept up their steady tugs on her nipples. The teasing sensations they created were driving her mad. Making her impatient. She wanted to come, and she wanted relief now.

She whimpered and moaned as pleasure increased and tightened through her lower belly. The arousal splashing around her made her feverish. Made her flesh sensitive to every touch they gave. The mouths at her breasts tugged harder on her nipples. She creamed some more.

Landon moaned. The dildo slid out of her clenching vagina, and the instant his succulent mouth fused over her aching pussy, she exploded on a scream, her body twisting against the restraints, her hips bucking against Landon's mouth.

Exquisite. Sheer bliss. This is it. This is what I've been craving. The mouths on her breasts increased their pressure. Tongues zapped her nipples. She tensed at the stirrings of the oncoming orgasm. Sensed it would be big and it would rock her. She wasn't mistaken.

Oh God!

The bliss enveloped her, rocked her to her very core. She shuddered and shook, trembled and gasped. She loved the pleasure. Accepted it. Drowned in it. Inhaled it deeply into her body.

Oh wow, this was better than she'd ever imagined. It was fantastic.

She bucked and held onto the erotic sensations for as long as she could, but too soon they ebbed away, her pussy spasming gently.

Then she was moaning in protest as all their touches suddenly stopped, and they were moving away from her.

God help her! They were moving away!

Nooo, don't leave me like this. She felt as if she were being twisted between pleasure and torture because her body ached in places she swore she'd never ached in before. She sensed the men moving away from her. Then the bed bounced and she cried out as her restraints were loosened. She was free, but not for long. Gentle, yet firm hands were grabbing her. Helping her to sit up.

"We're going to get you to lie on your tummy, Brandy." Landon soothed as he and someone else cradled her by her waist.

She moaned as someone kissed her. A hot, firm, wet kiss that sent her thoughts reeling. She didn't think it was Durango kissing her. Wasn't even sure it was Landon. She sensed it was Tyrell because of the big curvy chest muscles she could feel pressing against her left arm as he leaned into her. Tyrell's muscles were bigger than the other two's. And he smelled like cedar and spice. Yes, it had to be Tyrell.

His breaths were rough, his tongue bold, as he slammed past her lips and into her mouth. She met him full force and their tongues dueled and she was whimpering again, loving the feel of his flesh probing the inside of her mouth. Then all too soon, he was gone, his tongue darting out of her mouth.

"Nice, very nice, Liz." Tyrell breathed, and her lower belly clenched as he palmed her breast, testing its weight. She gasped and creamed as he flicked a finger across her tender, aching nipple. Then both her nipples were being flicked. It hurt. But the pain was a good hurt. Her nipples felt hot under the harsh taps. But she loved it. Loved feeling as if she were just two hot nipples. Two swollen breasts.

"She likes this, Durango," Tyrell said softly. "We'll have to do this every time."

"She likes everything we do to her. Don't you, Doc?" Durango breathed from somewhere near the foot of the bed. At least she thought it was near the foot of the bed. She wasn't too sure. She made a move to lift the blindfold, but a hand gripped her right wrist.

"Not yet, Brandy. Let Tyrell position some pillows for you so we can see your lovely ass. We need to remove the plug, remember?"

Liz nodded jerkily. Yes, they would have to take out the plug. Oh God, and then one of them would take her there.

She yelped as a palm smoothed along the inside of her right thigh, and automatically she opened her legs wider for whoever was touching her. Every touch was like a spark, and she was so aware of everything now.

Their scents. Their heavy breathing. The erotic way they touched her.

Three fingers dipped into her wet vagina, and she moaned at the naughty intrusion, her tummy clenching and her pussy spasming around the invasion.

"Yeah, very wet, aren't you, Doc? I know you better than you know yourself, sweet baby, Doc."

Durango.

"Damn you," she hissed and quickly shut up as he withdrew.

Disappointment slammed into her. She wanted his fingers inside her again. Thrusting. Plunging. Fucking.

She whimpered her frustration, and the two men holding her guided her onto her stomach. Pillows pushed up against her belly as she lay back down. And then they were restraining her again. The erotic feel of binds wrapping around her wrists and ankles had her moaning beneath the sultry sensations of anticipation snapping through her body. What would they do next?

* * * *

Durango burned for her. He could tell the other two men were having the same reaction. Their attentions were focused solely on her as if each one felt like he was alone in the room with her. Feeling that, he also knew each man had his own fetishes, his own desire where Doc was concerned.

He'd handpicked the men well. Knew their intimate desires. Knew Doc's desires. Yes, three of them would be a good fit for Doc, and he meant that literally.

He watched her cute ass clench as the guys tied her down again. He noticed the base of the plug bobbing ever so slightly, as those tight anal muscles clenched the toy.

His gut tightened with want. His cock felt ultraheavy with arousal and the intense need for release. But he knew the waiting for her would be worth this sheer agony. It was an agreement the three men shared. A pact they'd made. Her pleasure always came first. It meant whenever one of them wanted to take her, he would have to make sure he aroused her first. Make sure she craved the same sexual heat as the man wanting to take her. That way, she would anticipate being taken by one, two, or three of them.

As Tyrell and Landon completed their mission in tying her down, Tyrell moved onto the bed. Climbing sideways over her back, he lowered his hips, allowing the tip of his engorged cockhead to smooth over her upper back.

Liz tensed, her head moving sideways into curious mode. Tyrell grinned and winked at Durango, then groaned softly as he gyrated his hips, moving in such a fashion where Liz could feel the brand of his full shaft.

She whimpered, cried out softly with anticipation.

Durango's pulse pounded at a magnificent speed as he peered between Tyrell and Liz's body to watch Landon. The acrobatic son of a bitch crawled to the head of the bed where he sat down against the headboard, positioning himself in front of Liz's head. His legs stretched out to each side of her. He pulled his knees up, his heels digging into the mattress. Gently, Landon positioned her head so that her chin and the front of her neck rested on a low pillow.

Obviously Landon wanted Liz to go down on him again, and was using this position to take pressure off his injured thigh. Clever, that boy.

Durango's gut clenched as he heard Landon instruct her to open her mouth so he could slide himself into her. He discovered he was panting as he watched the two men play out their own fantasies with Liz, teasing her taut body with their own bodies. Anticipation continued to roar through him, and his fingers trembled as he grabbed the blue wooden paddle from the nearby dresser. Without hesitation he brought it down with a sharp slap upon her smooth, pale pink flesh. She bucked against the pain and moaned around Landon's thick cock.

"I guess you knew that was coming, didn't you, Doc?" he said softly as he caressed his palm over the pink flush he'd just created on her left ass cheek.

"And I know how much you enjoy it when I spank you, too." He smacked her again and enjoyed the erotic way her body writhed against the restraints.

A gurgled groan erupted from around Landon's shaft. He grinned, smacked the paddle against her flesh again and again, and loved watching how her ass clenched and the pink went into a deeper shade. Her reddening ass always turned him on so bad. Now, watching two men using her body to arouse themselves, he was ready to explode. Before long, a fine sheen of perspiration appeared on her lithe body, and he knew it would soon be time for all three of them to take her.

* * * *

Liz couldn't believe how wonderfully her body was responding to what the three men were doing to her. The hot brand of Tyrell's cock lacing her upper back and her mouth, full of Landon's flesh, had her simply writhing in excitement. Pain screamed through her scalp as one of the men, probably Landon, grabbed her hair, holding her steady. Gosh, who knew she could get so aroused at having her hair pulled? Unbelievable.

"Keep sucking, Brandy," Landon instructed. His voice sounded hoarse and strangled. The solid flesh in her mouth felt heavy and pulsing. She was sweating and trembling as her body reacted to what they were doing to her.

Heat coiled through her ass as Durango spanked her. The sensual heat spread outward into her pussy, up her belly and around her back to where Tyrell's cock rubbed all over her.

Pleasure rushed through her system at lightning speed, and her body was tightening as a climax began to roar toward her. Her lips felt swollen and tingled where she slurped and sucked on Landon's heavy, swollen erection, and the heavy cock rubbing along her back tickled her.

She would come soon. She had to. The heat was building inside of her. The tension was fraying her nerve endings. She was panting by the time Durango stopped spanking her. Her ass felt as if it was literally on fire, and she was creaming so badly she could barely stand this anymore.

It was awesome. Way too good. She was slipping into a world where nothing else existed. No self-control. No self-doubt about her sexuality. This is where she wanted to be. In her bed. Three men touching her. Her, simply existing.

She twisted as Durango smacked her behind again. The hardest yet, and she knew from previous experience it wouldn't be long before he took her. There was only so much Durango could take before he caved.

Her anticipation roared. The three of them would take her. They had to. She would go crazy if they didn't.

"We're almost there, Liz," Tyrell cooed from above her. "Man, you should see how your ass is blushing. You should see how Durango is so hard for you. I've never seen a man so hard for a lady before."

Liz whimpered as Tyrell's words dripped around her. God, she needed to see Durango. Wanted to see all of them. Wanted them.

She flinched, but continued sucking on Landon's cock as she became hotly aware of the butt plug being pulled from her. Durango. He was ready. He had to be.

Coils of heat snapped through her body as she waited with an eagerness she swore she'd never experienced before. She forced herself to relax. Calming herself would loosen her muscles' grip on the toy.

"That's it, baby doll. Just relax," Durango whispered.

The pressure mounted as the largest part of the plug passed her tight sphincter muscles and it left her with a loud pop. Liz trembled as she heard the slurp of lube and then a moment later felt a lubed finger enter her.

Durango groaned. "Nice and tight, Doc. We're going to have a field day back here when you take her, boys."

Hurry! Her mind screamed, the tension searing into her now.

Tyrell had moved himself away, and Landon was telling her to open her mouth so he could pull free.

Sweet mercy. Hurry. She tried to keep herself calm, but the finger exploring her ass felt so erotic.

The restraints were being loosened as a second lubed finger dipped into her ass. She whimpered at the gentle, too leisurely way he explored her back there. She knew he sensed her eagerness, her strain of need.

"Making sure you're sweetly lubed, Doc. We don't want to unnecessarily hurt you, right?"

"Hurry. Just hurry. Take me. All of you. I need all of you."

She was breathing so hard. She could barely stand it. The restraints on her arms were now free, and she ignored the soreness as she reached up and yanked the blindfold free. It was almost dark in here now. The evening had descended.

At the nearby window she noticed the eerie green glow of the northern lights as they made their nightly appearance.

"We're moving as fast as we can, baby," Tyrell said from the dresser area.

She wanted to move, but Durango was still lubing her ass, so she could only lay here on her belly, waiting anxiously. The rip of foil pumped through the chilly night air. Condoms. They were getting their condoms ready.

Oh wow, this was killing her.

"She's ready. Let's take her, boys." Durango. His voice drenched with a lust she'd never heard before.

Someone helped her onto her knees. Tyrell.

Someone was lying down beside her on the far edge of the bed. Landon. His heavily muscled arms moved in the darkness, and she could see he was stroking his big erection. He was watching her. Breathing heavily, his chest was moving up and down like crazy, and she swore his eyes were literally glowing with lust while he studied her as if he were a predator and she his prey.

"Climb onto Landon, sweetness," Durango instructed.

She wasn't even thinking as she followed Durango's instruction and moved over the man. A man she barely knew. She did know she wanted him. Wanted his big cock buried deep inside of her.

Durango grabbed her waist, his two hands like brands of molten steel as he guided her over Landon. Squatting, she angled herself until Landon was able to penetrate her vagina. Then Durango's hands left her waist, and his strong fingers curled around her shoulders as he pushed her downward.

She inhaled softly as Landon's cock slid into her. His stiff, swollen flesh impaled her to the hilt. Then Durango was pushing her downward. She understood what he wanted and lowered herself, her breasts flattening against Landon's muscles, and her mouth immediately fusing over Landon's mouth. His lips were soft, yet firm. Demanding, yet tender as he kissed her. His hands smoothed over her back, and he held her tight to him, as if never wanting to let her go. She loved the tight embrace. Felt safe and wanted. Loved.

She moaned as Durango's lubed, condom-sheathed cock slid into her ass. The full pressure unbelievably beautiful, it brought tears to her eyes.

"Turn this way, angel," Tyrell whispered from her right side. She did as he asked. She realized he was squatting beside Landon and herself, sitting on the bed in such a way were she came face-to-face with his engorged cock.

Huge cock, she corrected herself. She opened her mouth and accepted him, his girth stretching her lips like they'd never been stretched before.

Goodness, but he was so big!

Gyrating her hips, she gasped at the erotic feel of being double penetrated. Of being sandwiched between two heavily muscled men. Both Landon and Durango were groaning, both bucking into her, the intensity of her arousal making her cry out against Tyrell's cock.

Soon all three of the men found a perfect rhythm for themselves. Landon thrust his hips, creating a heady friction against her clit as he stayed inside her. Durango began a luscious thrust in and out of her ass, and Tyrell pistoned into her mouth.

She grew feverish, and an orgasm snapped through her at white-hot speed, making her body tighten, making her spiral out of control and into the world where nothing existed but pleasure. Pure arousal.

They fucked her like that for what seemed like an eternity. Bringing her to the edge of climaxes, holding her back, and then letting her soar into another one. She cried as swollen hard flesh thrust into her mouth, into her ass, impaled her pussy. By the time they were finished with her she was gasping for breath, and exhaustion snapped at her limbs. Her body was so sensitized to what they'd been doing that the sheets and then the comforters they placed over her literally shocked her body back into arousal mode, and she knew if she hadn't felt so sensually dazed at the aftereffects of what had just happened, she'd be begging them for more.

She needed rest. Then she could ask for more. Lots more.

Liz curled against the first available hard, hot body and tucked her pillow closer beneath her neck. She slept.

Chapter Eight

Liz knew she was dreaming about the day the Catastrophe hit. Knew she didn't want to relive it, but as always, she was powerless to stop it. Helpless to stop the sadness that enveloped her at losing all of her patients. She struggled to push away the dark emotions. Tried to wake herself up, but she couldn't. Everything played out like a puzzle. Pieces here and there, jumbled, confused. And as always, she knew they would sort themselves out, and that horrible day everyone called the Catastrophe would play out.

After the Catastrophe, she'd mourned all her patients, going so far as to bordering on clinical depression. She dare not think about the old days and her dependency on electricity, restaurants, and frozen dinners. Or her dependency on a car.

Gosh, of everything she missed, she missed her car the most. But her car hadn't worked, just like all the rest of the cars Durango and she had tried to start. Durango had used his mechanic skills for months trying to get a vehicle going. Nothing worked.

Even vehicles that hadn't been running the day the solar flares hit didn't start. Durango had never been able to figure out why. No one had.

He'd tried to fix other modes of transportation that hadn't started either. He'd tried everything. Tractors, all-terrain vehicles, motor boats. Nothing worked. Not even a spark.

She didn't know the ins and outs of how the Catastrophe had played out, but the prevalent theory she'd heard was it had something to do with solar flares attacking people with certain types of genes. Those people had, according to witnesses, simply disintegrated after a flash of light had been seen in the sky. They'd turned into fireballs, self-combusting and ending up piles of ash wherever they'd been at the time the flares had erupted.

The flares had fried electrical grids, radio towers, satellites, some of which had fallen from the skies. Even airplanes had fallen out of the skies. Trains had crashed. Boats devoid of people had floated aimlessly in lakes and oceans.

She still remembered the day when their lives had changed. Durango and she had been having a magnificent bout of mid-afternoon sex. Their shades had been drawn, the room was pleasantly dark, and their central air conditioner had been pleasantly humming away, pumping out cool air that bathed their perspiration-soaked bodies. She'd been orgasming when she'd felt unusually hot for a second. Had vaguely noticed the central air stopping as she cried out her release.

After her orgasm, Durango had cradled her in his arms, and they'd lain quietly in bed, their breaths quick in the after-sex glow. It wasn't until maybe an hour or so later that Durango mentioned the central air wasn't working. She had forgotten about it after drifting off to sleep. She'd protested when he'd climbed out of bed, but he'd noted that it would start getting warm in here if he didn't get it started again.

He'd played around with the buttons for a couple of seconds before frowning. "Huh, not working. The digital here is blank. Ever had a problem with your central air before?" Durango asked as he sat back down on the bed and gazed at her. Even in the dimness of the room she could see the love shining in his eyes for her, and it melted her insides knowing this guy with the nice bulging muscles was all hers. She had the engagement ring to prove it.

He gazed at the clock on his side of the bed. "The digital clock isn't working either. Power must be out."

"Probably because everyone and their mother has cranked up their air cons, too. Or maybe we were just so hot that we fried the electricity?" she joked and laughed and realized it was getting stuffy in the room.

"Maybe we should let some air in?" She looked to the window.

He nodded in agreement. "Just a couple of minutes though. All that humidity is just gonna come in and ruin the remaining coolness."

She watched Durango get up and stroll across the room toward the window. His big cock was already at half-mast, and she knew it wouldn't be long before he wanted more sex. The man was killing her gently with all this sex.

Every weekend, it seemed, they spent in bed fucking each other's brains out. And every night too after they came from work and then sometimes in the mornings before they showered and took off for work, they had sex. In the shower. On the kitchen table. Even on the dryer.

He was a highly sexual man, and until meeting him, she hadn't realized how sexual she was either.

"I have to take a leak first," he said and did an about-face and headed into the adjoining bathroom. A couple of minutes later she heard the toilet flush and noticed it sounded funny as if there wasn't enough water pressure or something.

Great.

"Toilet's fucked, and so is the water. Meaning we don't have any. Must be one hell of a power failure."

Oh crap. She snuggled beneath the sheets and watched as he strolled to the window and lifted the shade. Sunshine washed into the room, the brightness hurting her eyes.

"What the fuck?" Durango said as he looked out the window. Something in his voice, maybe fear, or surprise, or both, sent creepy shivers of dread up her spine.

"Come here, Doc. Take a look at this."

She joined him, grabbing a sheet from the bed and covering herself. Gazing out the upstairs bedroom window, Liz could still feel how hard and fast the disbelief had shifted through her like an evil snake.

Everything looked the same, but it looked different, too. She couldn't put a finger on it, but the sky seemed to have changed to a deeper blue, and the air was breezy and cold. But just this morning she'd listened to the weather forecast, and they'd been predicting hot, humid, and hazy weather for at least another week with no relief in sight beyond that.

She hugged the sheet tighter around her and shivered at the cold onslaught. "Obviously the weather guys fucked up again," she complained.

"Forget the weather, what the fuck is going on down on the street?"

Liz's gaze dropped to the street which, usually teeming with people strolling toward the park down the road, was totally empty. Not only that, she noticed a couple of cars parked precariously on people's lawns. One car was even parked in front of their neighbor's house on the lawn directly across the street from them. The car had climbed the curb and come to rest in Carol's flower bed and snapped their treasured Austrian pine tree right in half.

"Carol's gonna be pissed," Liz commented.

"I'm gonna call Bill and see what happened."

Durango lifted the receiver and slammed it down. He grinned at her, obviously trying to play it cool, and her heart flip flopped all over the place. Such a sexy smile. She wanted to tell him to screw the phones and get back to fucking her, but he was already reaching for his jeans on the floor.

"No dial tone. Good thing we have cell phones."

She glanced back outside and noticed a ribbon of black smoke around a mile to the north. The airport was up that way. In the distance she noticed a couple more spirals of dark smoke. Weird.

"Something's on fire out there. And it's way too quiet, too. Where are all the people?"

"My cell phone is totally dead. So is yours," Durango said as he joined her at the window and peered out.

"Yeah, looks like something is on fire in a few places. I want you to stay here while I go over to Bob and Carol's. Better check on what's going on with that car running up their tree, too. Maybe they know what's happened."

"Something's not right," she whispered as icy shivers began crawling up her spine again.

A frown dropped onto his face again, and she silently willed him to smile. He didn't.

"It's okay. Just stay here, okay?"

"Yeah, sure." Truth was, she'd kind of gotten the creeps and preferred to stay here where it felt…normal.

He grabbed his shirt, and a couple of minutes later, she watched from the window as he strolled across the street to the car that sat on Bob and Carol's lawn. He peered in the vehicle's windows. Something must have alarmed him because he'd quickly looked up at her and waved his hand signaling to her to stay put. She'd watched as he knocked on Bob and Carol's front door and waited. He knocked a couple of more times, and then surprisingly he'd opened the door and disappeared inside the building.

Her gaze drifted to the increasing number of plumes of black smoke. She darted a look up and down the street. No traffic. No people. What the fuck was going on?

She reached for the clock radio on the bedside table and flicked it on. Silence. Shit! She'd forgotten the electricity had gone out.

Okay, so this was not good. Not good at all. She snapped through her memory trying to figure out where she'd put her watch. She found it on the dresser. It had died, too.

What the fuck?

A few moments later, Durango had returned and their nightmare had begun…

Liz awoke with a jolt, her heart hammering and cold perspiration clinging to her clammy skin. She bit her bottom lip and forced herself to steady her breathing.

Just a nightmare. She wasn't back in Calgary. She wasn't reliving the Catastrophe. She was here, safe and sound, in this little century-old stone house. Durango was here and Landon and Tyrell. Everything was fine.

She burrowed deeper against her pillows and clutched the comforters tighter over her chilled body. Ignoring the gentle throbbing in her butt and pussy, she smiled. Yeah, she'd liked what had happened last night. Liked it a lot.

* * * *

"When the time comes for us to leave, I'm staying," Landon said. He was perfectly prepared to fight Tyrell and Durango on this matter, and he was surprised when Tyrell nodded his head and Durango didn't so much as say a word of protest as he broke breakfast eggs and set them onto the frying pan of the woodstove Liz had in the kitchen.

"I'm not leaving her either," Tyrell said from his perch where he stood on a kitchen stool, frantically searching the upper cabinet for some pepper. Tyrell loved his eggs sunny-side up and doused in pepper. Unfortunately these days pepper was virtually impossible to buy.

Eggs, on the other hand, were plentiful, since everyone and their mother seemed to pay Liz for her doctoring services with eggs instead of money.

"No one's going anywhere. It's not safe for Liz to be here alone any longer," Durango said as he sprinkled salt onto the eggs.

Durango's words diffused the pent-up anger Landon had been harboring ever since he'd awoken this morning. The three of them had roused around the same time and left Liz still fast asleep, despite the fact all of them wanted to take her again.

The woman was just perfect, Landon thought as he remembered how she'd eagerly kissed him and allowed Durango to guide her over his erection, effectively impaling her on him.

Man, she'd been so tight. Her kisses so hot and passionate, and her sweet body convulsing all over the place every time she'd orgasmed.

He knew he loved her from the moment Durango had brought him here. Knew he would die protecting her if and when the time came.

"What about the gang? Aren't they going to be pissed?" Tyrell asked as he stumbled off the stool and headed for the pantry.

"I've already sent word through Logan," Durango replied. "Told him yesterday when I was helping them. He volunteered to take a ride up and tell the guys. I'm sure they'll understand."

"Geez, first there were nine of us in the gang, and now only three left." Landon laughed, but then blades of seriousness flowed through him as he focused his attention on Durango. "Are you going to be able to handle the boredom of surviving day by day, Durango? It ate you up the last time, to the point where you were snapping Liz's and my heads off."

There was a glint of excitement Landon had never seen in Durango's eyes before as the man smiled. "That's before I realized we can survive without the use of stores and cities, gentlemen. Despite this cold weather we are going to go into the farm business. We are going to become self-sufficient. If our neighbors Teyla and Logan and the guys can do it via a greenhouse, then we can, too. With animals." Durango smiled at the two of them, and Landon could literally feel the man's excitement zipping through him as well.

Durango continued. "And when we become self-sufficient, we're going to become self-employed. How's that sound? No more bosses. No more robberies. No more posses. Just us running everything ourselves and keeping prices reasonable so we can stay in business, but so we can also help out the people who most need it. Since every son of a bitch is out there charging so much for everything, we'll undercut them and put them right out of business, compliments of their greediness."

Landon nodded. "We can start by getting our hands on some wild chickens and rabbits. Knock together some buildings and house them. Chickens need warmth to keep producing eggs. So we'll create that environment. It'll take time to get the supplies, but with all the abandoned homes and farms in the valleys we should be able to piece together what we'll need."

Tyrell chuckled as he pulled out a small tin of pepper. "Yes! Liz is my kind of woman. She must love pepper on her eggs, too. She's got a good stock of food in here, too."

"She gets it from the clients she treats," Durango replied as he grabbed a spatula from a nearby pitcher containing such utensils.

Landon grinned. "Perfect. Liz loves to cook when she's nervous. With the three of us around, she'll be nervous wondering when one of us wants to take her, so she'll be doing a lot of cooking."

"A way to a man's heart is through his stomach," Tyrell said as he plopped down in his seat at the kitchen table, pepper tin ready in hand while Durango slid a couple of eggs onto his plate.

Yep, Tyrell was definitely on the mend if he could have sex with Liz so much last night without busting a stitch in his side wound and now getting happy over some freaking pepper.

"In the meantime, we can see if we can rent some greenhouse space from Teyla to grow some of the greens the animals will need." Durango kept talking, but Landon began tuning him out as he spied movement in the hallway.

He looked up and surprise washed through him at seeing Liz standing there. In a split second, Landon forgot how to breathe. She looked spectacular. Her cheeks were flushed, her eyes were fever bright with arousal, and her pretty honey-blonde hair shone brightly in the early morning sunshine streaming in through the kitchen windows.

She also looked quite shy with her hands twisted nervously together in front of her as she watched them in the kitchen. When she saw him watching her, she smiled and the cutest dimples popped out in her cheeks. He swore his heart burst at the seams with happiness.

"I...I was hungry...I mean...um for food," she said softly.

Upon hearing her sweet voice, Tyrell and Durango whirled around. Landon swore Tyrell's cheeks blushed the slightest shade of pink, and Durango almost dropped the frying pan. The two men didn't move an inch and simply stared at her as if transfixed by her beauty.

Landon shook his head. These guys were suddenly acting like a couple of starstruck teenagers.

"Come on, guys, give the lady a seat. She needs food. Serve her." He was at her side within two quick strides, and grabbing her hand, he led her to a seat beside Tyrell, who actually stood while Landon seated her.

Fuck. Looked like chivalry wasn't dead these days. Who would have guessed Tyrell would be so smitten with her?

"Here you go, baby. Some eggs to get some energy into you. You're going to need it." Her eyes widened at Durango's comment, and Landon noticed a look of alarm splashing over her face.

"Give the girl a break. She needs to rest after last night," Landon soothed. The way the two of them were drooling as they stared at her, she probably thought the three of them were sex maniacs demanding sex before she even had breakfast. But Durango was right. She needed the energy because he was dying to take her again. But he'd be a gentleman and wait until after breakfast.

* * * *

Durango watched the two men gazing longingly at Liz while all four of them ate. Conversation was quiet and restricted to requests to pass the salt and pepper, to the weather outside which looked sunnier and more cheerful than ever. Of course that could be just him due to the fact he noticed a soft, satisfied smile curving the sides of Liz's sensually shaped mouth as she shot quick glances at Durango.

He knew she wanted to speak privately to him. Could understand it in the way her eyes twinkled so brightly as if she were bursting with barely restrained excitement. Or maybe he was reading her wrong? Maybe the excitement had everything to do with her anticipating them taking her after breakfast?

That idea, of course, made his cock grow just that much harder, and it was harder than a son of a bitch already after awakening this morning and feeling her warm body pressed snugly against him. Funny thing was he hadn't heard those sensual whimpers that she'd kept having every night until he'd finally left to join the Durango Gang. Those erotic sounds had tormented him into many sleepless nights, and last night he hadn't heard a thing.

Unless, of course, she'd stopped with her fantasy dreams after he'd left? Durango shook his head and shoved the last forkful of egg into his mouth. No, he could read a woman, and instincts told him she was finally satisfied with three men fucking her. Hell, he was satisfied, too.

"Were you serious?" Liz said shyly as she reached for the mug of coffee Tyrell had brewed up for all of them in the antique percolator on the woodstove. Liz was staring straight at him, so it was obvious the question was aimed at him.

"About?"

"You staying. You all staying."

He'd been pretty sure she'd heard their conversation, but maybe she just needed to hear it from him.

"Yes. We won't be leaving you again. Except, of course, on short trips to forage abandoned houses and barns for the supplies we'll need to get us self-sufficient. In the meantime, Doc, we're going to need to sponge food off you until we can set things up. Is that okay with you?"

She was smiling, and his heart squeezed with excitement. Yeah, she sure did look pretty when she smiled.

"I don't have much, but please consider what I have as yours." Her gaze widened to Landon and Tyrell. "All of you."

The men's breaths were starting to speed up, and Durango knew he needed to get the guys out of the kitchen before they started in on another ménage. She needed to get washed up, and he needed to make sure she was really okay with all this, now that she had an idea of what was involved.

"Boys. Around back of the house, you'll find a bathtub in a lean-to. There's a pump and lots of pails plus a drum-style wood-burning stove. Doc would appreciate it if you set her up with a nice hot bath."

Landon and Tyrell nodded eagerly, and they both tried to outrun each other as they headed into the living room. A moment later they both popped back with jackets in hand and headed down the hallway. A few seconds later they heard the back door slam shut.

Silence followed.

* * * *

Liz couldn't express the rush of excitement racing rampant through her at Durango confirming he was staying. Obviously he'd found what he'd been searching for over the last few months, or maybe it had just been an "absence makes the heart grow fonder" kind of thing. Who knew. Who cared. He was staying. Landon was staying, and she sensed this new fellow, Tyrell, would be additional icing on an already very sweet and yummy cake.

She shivered as he moved his chair right beside hers. His body heat splashed all around her, making her very conscious of him. Gosh, she'd always been so aware of him, and now with him back after all this time, the awareness had grown exponentially.

"You enjoyed last night?" he asked softly.

She could read the hope in his eyes. The need for her to finally admit that, yeah, she enjoyed having sex with more than one man, just as much as he enjoyed watching her with them.

God, of all the guys, she'd have to fall in love with a mechanic whose body was laced with awesome muscles, and who enjoyed sharing his woman. She wondered what would have happened if she'd never met him. Would her sexually submissive side have come to light? Or would it have stayed hidden beneath the modern morals she'd been brought up with? Thankfully she would never know, because she wanted to be dominated.

She wanted to be taken whenever *someone else* wanted to take her. She loved the anticipation of it. The erotic way it made her feel, just knowing a man wanted her. It made her feel...desirable.

Low self-esteem issues? No, she didn't think so. She felt good about herself, about what she'd achieved in life. Becoming a doctor had taken all of her self-discipline to achieve her dream. But in doing so, she'd ignored her private life. Ignored her needs. Now she wanted to explore those cravings burning inside her.

She also knew that just because both she and Durango had kinky needs didn't mean their relationship was meant to be. It meant they were a good fit. At least that's what she thought. She could make his fantasies of sharing come true, and he could make her fantasies of ménages and being dominated by more than one man come true.

Now with the removal of the social elements due to the Catastrophe, she was realizing there was a new type of freedom available to her. Her family couldn't judge her. Pretty much all of her friends were dead, and her one true friend, Teyla, was living out Liz's dream only a couple of miles away. She'd so envied Teyla that she'd been barely able to stand it.

"I really missed you, Doc," Durango whispered as he took her hands into his. "I woke up aching for you every night. Kept dreaming about how sweet you would taste when I came back home. How I longed to bring you the pleasure I knew you craved. We both craved."

And the pleasure she denied she needed.

"Now that you've had a taste, do you want what the three of us are offering?"

Hope glittered with such magnificence in his gaze that Liz swore if she hadn't been sitting her on the chair, her knees would have buckled from the intensity. That Durango would even ask her instead of seducing sex from her again meant he'd turned a serious curve in the road of seduction. She sensed if she said no, he would accept her decision. And maybe leave like he'd done before?

She hoped the threat of him leaving wasn't what was influencing her decision to give in to what he wanted. No, it was what *she* wanted. She needed to remember that. It had to be what she wanted because in the end she would be living with the consequences, despite having no family or friends to judge her. She had to be comfortable with her decisions.

"This isn't something I can just agree to, Durango."

Hope deflated in his eyes. She felt bad, truly she did, but what he'd given her a taste of was an entire change of life for her. Being here for three men who she would sexually submit to whenever they wanted. God, just thinking about it was turning her on big-time.

She licked her lips, tried to quell the visions of what had happened last night. Being tied down, three men fucking her. It had been awesome, and she realized she was truly beginning to accept this idea.

"I can't be at every man's beck and call in the bedroom and out. Things need to be done, like preparation of meals, house work, yard work, farming. I can't help with all that if I'm lying in bed all the time getting my brains screwed out." *And loving it.*

"It won't be in the bed, always," he teased and leaned in. She shivered as he brushed his mouth against her lips again in a feather-like kiss.

"Durango, I'm serious."

He pulled away, a gorgeous grin tipping the sides of his luscious-looking mouth. A mouth she wouldn't mind having between her legs at the moment. Her lower belly clenched at the thought of his early morning shadow brushing erotically against her inner thighs.

Oh goodness, they'd turned her into a sex maniac already. Liz blinked that thought aside.

"All three of us have two arms and hands, Doc. We know how to do housework. It's not just a woman's job. We are modern men. We'll make up a schedule of chores for all three guys."

"Domesticated already," she teased.

"Doc, for you, anything. I love you. I need you. You are the lifeblood that runs through my veins, baby. I realized that when I left. I was a stubborn fool for not coming back sooner."

"Yes, you are."

His grin widened. "As opposed to *I was*. Not past tense?"

Happiness bubbled through her at his teasing. Lifting her arms, she wrapped them around his neck and curled her fingers against the back of his head.

His eyes twinkled. He had the most beautiful eyes. It was like looking into the dark blue sky at twilight.

"I have demands, too. I have needs," she began as she remembered what Teyla had told her when she'd been here for a visit yesterday.

"Lots of needs," he whispered and brushed his mouth against hers in an intoxicating featherlight kiss that had her breaths increasing in speed.

"The agreement goes both ways. When I want a man to submit to me, then he must. Or all three of you for that matter."

There was an explosion of emotions in his eyes, and for a second Liz swore she forgot to breathe. She could read the emotions clearly. Excitement. Arousal. Want. They all swirled like a tornado threatening to suck her right up.

"And I want something from you right now," she said softly.

She felt him tense against her. Saw him lick his lips in anticipation.

"Anything, baby, anything."

"Go outside and help Tyrell and Landon fill the tub. I'm dying for a hot bath."

His face flopped into disappointment. She wiggled her fingers against the back of his head and struggled to keep a straight face as she knew he'd been expecting her to say, "Let's have sex."

"Can you do that for me, honey? Help the guys draw a nice hot bath for me? Oh, and when you're finished with that, there's more wood that needs chopping so that tomorrow morning when I need my bath, the wood will be there for you to toss into the drum stove."

His frown deepened, and she seriously wanted to start laughing. The man still had to learn to put his money where his mouth was, didn't he? Oh well, training him and the other three would be fun.

"Oh, and after my bath, I want you guys to get right on a 'honey do this' list for all three of you. I want you to figure out who is going to do housework and what chores you guys prefer to have. You may as well take the ones you enjoy the most. Each of you. Then at least they'll get done if you enjoy doing them."

She ignored his raised eyebrows and the puzzlement on his face, stood, and headed for the hallway. She expected him to protest, to demand she get back into the kitchen and have sex with him. He didn't, and oddly enough she was disappointed. But yeah, Teyla was right. Liz needed to make demands of her own from the three men, and now would be the time to start.

Slipping into the bedroom, she closed the door behind her, and a couple of minutes later she heard the front door creak open as Durango left the house. Moments after that, she heard the men talking behind the house in the general direction of where the outdoor tub was located. Then she heard the sound of someone chopping wood.

Liz smiled. Huh, that was easy.

Too easy, a voice warned as she began to gather the things she would need for her much-anticipated bath.

Way too easy.

Chapter Nine

When Liz let herself out the back door, cold mid-morning air blasted against her. She gripped the bathrobe tighter around her and quickly walked toward the lean-to that housed the bathtub. Before leaving to join Durango's cousin's gang, Durango and Landon had built the lean-to with the opening facing south, allowing for a sunny exposure while she bathed. They'd found the claw foot tub in one of the desolate farmhouses in the valley, as well as a handmade woodstove made from a drum at another neighboring farm. They'd lugged the items here to her place. Now, as she strolled across the meadow toward the lean-to, she smelled the aroma of wood smoke, saw the grey smoke spiraling lazily from the long pipe attached to the stove, but none of the men were in sight.

Where had they gotten off to? She set her towel, the bar of lavender-scented soap, and a disposable razor onto the wood shelf within reach. She gazed at the tub and laughed with enjoyment. They'd filled it to almost the rim. Lots of hot baths. Hmm, another benefit of having three strong men here with her. So, she traded it off with some hot and heavy sex. How could anything be wrong with that?

Disrobing, she shivered in the cold air and quickly stepped into the high tub, sighing as she sat into hot liquid heaven. Water embraced her sore pussy, ass, and her tender breasts, lapping against all those muscles she never knew she had. Oh yeah, she could get used to having wonderful hot baths every morning.

Grabbing the soap, she quickly washed her hair and the rest of her, taking extra care to soap her tender breasts, pussy, and other intimate area. She would need to be clean for the guys.

Smiling, she remembered last night. It had felt wonderful being impaled on Landon and having Durango thrusting into her tender ass while Tyrell fucked her mouth. Just thinking about the pleasure they'd created, had her moaning softly and closing her eyes.

Yes, this new way of life could certainly turn into paradise. Licking her lips in anticipation, she ran a hand leisurely over her sensitized breasts, surprised at the need gripping her with such a fierce intensity she hadn't felt before. Smoothing her other hand down over her lower belly, she ran a finger between her labia to rub her clit. Her pussy and ass both clenched hard, and she moaned softly at the reaction.

Oh lovely. She was seriously arousing herself and not a man in sight to bring her relief.

As she continued touching herself, she turned her face into the cold breeze and warm sunshine. Thankfully the lean-to blocked most of the wind, and the smoke from the nearby woodstove was minimal as it escaped the tall pipe. She could hear the wood crackling in the stove and listened to the wind whistle through the nearby tall grass.

She sunk deeper into the tub, sighing as the warm water embraced her body. Steam curled around in front of her eyes, and lavender-scented soap wafted off her skin making her feel as if she were a queen soaking in a tub awaiting her male sex slaves to approach her and make love to her.

She closed her eyes and smiled at that idea. She gasped as she pinched her nipples, finding them tender as well. Those men sure had known what they'd been doing last night, and she wouldn't have traded that experience for the world. Now that she'd stepped over the threshold, she doubted she would want to go back to living alone. Now, she understood what her friend Teyla had meant when she'd told Liz the same thing. Menages were addictive.

She sensed the men before she even opened her eyes. Knew the three of them had come for her. Knew she wouldn't say no. Could never say no to the pleasure they were sure to give her.

Slowly, she opened her eyes, and blinked at the three men who stood around the tub staring down at her naked form lounging in the water. She didn't even feel a spark of shame at being caught like this, nude and touching herself. She felt as if she were Alice in Wonderland and she'd slipped down the rabbit's hole, appearing in a new world. A world she wanted. One she knew she would like.

"You looked too luscious for us to ignore, Doc," Durango whispered. His voice sounded hoarse and strangled. Aroused. His eyes were the deepest blue she'd ever seen them, and there was a sparkle of amusement in his gaze.

"We made up that honey-do list you were mentioning earlier to Durango," Landon said as he, too, gazed down at her body. Liz stilled at his intense look, and succulent heat fused through her.

She tried to concentrate on what Landon had just said. The honey-do list? And then she remembered. Oh great, Durango had mentioned their earlier conversation to them? Would anything she said be a secret between the two of them? Somehow she doubted it. These three men had formed a tight bond, and she would be their woman. She'd better get used to it and fast.

Her gaze drifted to Tyrell. A luscious smile tilted the tips of his lips, and she had the distinct feeling he had a secret. They all had a secret.

"Okay, what's up?" she asked, liking their playful looks.

Tyrell lifted a piece of paper and handed it down to her. Water dripped from her arm as she accepted it and read what they'd written.

It was the honey-do list she'd been talking to Durango about. The men had made up a schedule in record time, outlining all the chores each of them would do. Amazing.

"I'm impressed," Liz said as she read the neatly scrawled handwriting.

"You also mentioned you had needs, Brandy," Landon said softly.

"We figured with the way you're touching yourself, we would come in handy about now," Tyrell whispered.

"I want to watch," Durango added.

Liz swallowed, felt the familiar rush of lust shifting through her like a drug as the three men peered at her with way too much anticipation.

"Since when do you guys have to ask?" she replied, handing the note back to Tyrell.

"We're not asking, babe," Durango replied hoarsely.

Liz trembled at the domination in his voice.

"We made an adjustment to the lean-to while you were inside," Tyrell said, his gaze moving upward. Liz followed to where he was looking, and she started. Directly above the tub, on a beam in the ceiling of the lean-to, she caught a glimpse of silver. A large eye bolt had been screwed into the wood beam. From it hung a hook.

Her breathing quickened. Why hadn't she seen that up there? Because she'd been too busy pleasuring herself, that was why.

She looked back down and met Durango's gaze, read the sexual intent flaring in his blue eyes. Her breath caught at the heated look, at the sizzling tension zipping between the two of them. She grew so hot she was surprised the water hadn't started to boil. He held up some long leather straps with cuffs.

She creamed. Hard. She knew what was going on. Leather straps and attachments. They would bind her. This time they would take her while she was standing.

She licked her lips as a sensual nervousness zipped through her. Shivered as the intense yearning to have sex with them took hold with a vengeance.

"We have needs, too, Brandy," Landon said as he leisurely removed his jacket and hung it on one of several nail posts. He began to undress.

"Lots of needs, Elizabeth," Tyrell replied as he, too, removed his jacket and hung it beside Landon's. He began to undress.

Oh my gosh.

She fought her growing nervousness as Durango didn't move. Didn't undress. Instead, he leaned over the bathtub, his hand slipping into the water. She thought he would start stroking her pussy, but his hand wrapped around her wrist like a taut rope.

"Stand, baby." His gaze riveted her. Hot waves of pure sensuality blazed off his body into hers.

"Stand for them," he whispered.

He wanted her to stand so he could watch her be taken by the other two. She knew he did. That's why he wasn't getting undressed.

"Durango..." she whispered, suddenly feeling unsure of this. Maybe she wasn't able to get into this new lifestyle? Maybe this situation was impossible? She already liked Landon a lot, and Tyrell was so nice, but she didn't really know these two. Durango wanted all of them living here like some polygamous family or something. What if they decided they didn't want her anymore?

Fear and self-doubt almost devoured her, but then she looked into Durango's eyes and saw the love flaming there for her. Love, lust, and appreciation for what she was going to give him.

"It's okay, baby. It's okay," he soothed. Obviously he was sensing her uneasiness.

No, he would never leave her again. She knew that now. He'd gone away and he'd come back. And she wanted this.

Confidence pushed away her wariness. It felt good. She felt good. This was right. This is what she wanted.

Durango tugged and she managed to get up out of the water and stand in the tub on her trembling legs. Cold air breathed against her wet flesh, but the coldness only heightened her arousal. Water dripped off her shivering body, and she whimpered as he strapped the cuffs securely around each wrist. Then he lifted her arms way up over her head, and she watched helplessly as he hooked the restraints above.

She was trapped. At his mercy again. At their mercy again. She felt overheated with the excitement. Burning with the anticipation of being taken. Of being sandwiched between two hard, muscular bodies.

As Durango held her gaze, she heard the rustling of clothing being removed. Heard the slurp of lube.

Oh God.

Durango was breathing hard as he drew away and allowed the other two men, totally naked now and both wearing condoms, to step into the tub with her. Tyrell in front. Landon in back.

She could feel their body heat coming at her from both sides. Waves of sensual heat wrapped around her, chasing away the chill. She could smell Tyrell. Sexy. Strong. Spicy. And Landon's scent. Pine, soap, and fresh air.

A strong pair of hands settled over the curves of her hips. Landon.

Corded muscles bunched in Tyrell's biceps as his hot hands slipped against her waist, holding her steady.

"You're the most beautiful woman I've ever come across, Elizabeth," Tyrell whispered. She knew he was lying. He had to be. But she liked his compliments.

"So sexy. I enjoyed watching what happened between you and Durango and Landon in the kitchen."

Her eyes widened in surprise. He'd seen them having sex. Heat cascaded through her, and her cheeks flushed. Great, now her cheeks were getting red, she just knew it.

He grinned, obviously enjoying her embarrassment. He licked his lower lip. Her gaze dropped to his tongue. He had a nice tongue. Red and perfect.

Behind her, Landon nuzzled against the curve of her neck and shoulder, his bristles erotically scratching her sensitive flesh.

"You don't even realize how sensual you are, do you, Brandy?" Landon murmured, and her body tingled as he lapped his tongue along her neck. "I like that about you. Being modest makes you even more beautiful."

She moaned as his large cockhead pressed between her butt cheeks and against her sphincter.

"Shh, you'll love this, sweetness. I promise." Tyrell bent his head, his mouth capturing hers in a firm, demanding kiss. She liked the taste of him. Dark and sensual, like coffee after a hot night of sex.

Automatically she widened her legs, catching her balance.

His mouth moved over hers confidently, his tongue pushing past the last remnants of her resistance. He lashed his tongue against hers. The connection was blistering. So intense, it snapped all her nerve endings on fire. His steel-hard cockhead rubbed firmly against her sensitive clit, sparking all kinds of wicked sensations. Her pussy clenched. Her ass throbbed with anticipation. Gosh, this felt so wonderful.

Liz shuddered, cried out as the pressure built in her ass and Landon slipped in with his generously lubed cock. Slid in easily, slowly, stretching her until she gasped into Tyrell's mouth at the immense invasion burrowing into her behind.

Tyrell's hands slipped off her waist and started roaming her body.

Landon pulled free, and without warning, Tyrell thrust into her vagina. Hot and heavy and so thick, his fiery shaft pistoned boldly into her, making her moan at the intensity of his size and quickness of his penetration.

Writhing now, she was sandwiched between their hard bodies. Coils of arousal uncurled quickly now, building and wrapping around her, making her gyrate her hips and buck against them.

"That's it, Brandy. Let's show Durango how you love being fucked by two men," Landon whispered against her neck, then kissed her there. Just the mention of Durango, the thought of him watching and enjoying his fantasy at her being fucked by two men, made her even more keyed up.

"Durango said you also like it rough. So do we," Tyrell whispered against her mouth, after breaking the intense kisses.

Tyrell withdrew his engorged shaft, and Landon's hip surged against hers as he thrust into her ass again. Immediately, the two picked up an intense rhythm, burying themselves inside her. Fire burned through her, and within moments she came apart.

She exploded on a cry, her body twisting against the restraints that held her captive. Her hips bucking between the two men as they entered her over and over again. Sensations rocked her. Tore through her like a tornado, and she went with it, her mind snapping, her body convulsing and accepting them into her being. Into her soul. Into her heart.

Perfect, something in the back of her mind whispered. Liz smiled. Yes, they were a perfect fit. And they were her home.

* * * *

Tyrell grinned against Elizabeth's mouth as he felt her come apart in his arms. Her body shivered and convulsed against him under the onslaught of her orgasm. She cried softly, erotically, the sexy sounds making him jerk his hips harder against her, every thrust harder and deeper, until the pleasure gripped his balls full force, lashed his cock, and ripped through him with fierce intensity.

The power of the impending climax just about had him dropping to his knees, but he held tight to her hips and continued holding the rhythm with Landon, waiting for him to come first. But Landon kept pistoning, obviously trying for a second orgasm for her. Hell, he could do that. He thrust harder, loving the way she gave back as much as he pushed at her.

Between them, she was panting. Her entire body trembled. Her cunt clenched around his shaft, holding his cock with a tremendous grip that her pussy was pretty much locking onto his shaft.

He tried to hold back the tidal wave of oncoming pleasure, but he just couldn't. He let go of his self-control and thrust harder.

Once. Twice. And then he exploded on a strangled shout as her viselike muscles clamped so hard, he couldn't stop himself from spilling.

He cried out her name at the same time as something really nice swelled inside his heart for her. He rocked with her, realizing he couldn't stop whispering her name.

"Elizabeth. Elizabeth." Such a pretty name. Such a beautiful woman.

Yeah, he was going to enjoy hanging out here with Durango and Landon. Building a business. A safe haven for them. Best of all, building a warm, loving home for Elizabeth.

* * * *

Landon had been waiting for Tyrell to climax. When he hadn't, Landon had been barely able to keep up his hard thrusts, he'd been so desperate to come.

Liz was perfect. Her tight muscles just about had him coming from the first moment he'd slid into her. But he was an unselfish gentleman when it came to women. Had always waited until his companion came before he joined her. He would extend that consideration to a second or a third, whatever the case would be. That's just the way he was.

Thankfully, Tyrell finally came. Landon knew it in the last few frantic thrusts against Liz. Heard it in Tyrell's increased pants and then the tormented way he began whispering her name as if it were a love chant.

Landon smiled, felt his heart crash open in gratitude to Durango and Liz for allowing him to be here with them. He finally had a place to call home, and her name was Brandy. He nuzzled his mouth against her warm neck, held tight to her waist, pulled out of her and plunged back into her succulent ass. Once. Twice. He bucked. Pleasure slammed through his cock and balls.

Three times.

He exploded. He couldn't help but groan in satisfaction as he twisted in the erotic throes of arousal as it embraced him head-on like intense blades of lightning. Yeah, he would like it here.

He was home.

* * * *

Durango came on a strangled cry as he joined the three in their combined release. Shards of shivers embraced him. The blades of pleasure ripped him apart with an intensity he'd never felt before. Watching Liz sandwiched between two men, their hard, strong bodies dominating hers, their powerful thrusts against her ripping erotic gasps out of her mouth, making her shudder and shake with fierce arousal, was something he'd always craved to see. It had been everything he'd ever wanted. For him and most of all, for her.

As if sensing him watching her, she suddenly opened her eyes and smiled at him. "I love this. I love you," she mouthed. She closed her eyes again, embracing the pleasure, and fierce happiness swept through him.

It was so obvious to him he hadn't been wrong about her. She'd just needed a little push in the direction where her cravings lie. She'd needed a shove to shed her inhibitions. She was shy right now, but it wouldn't be long before she hungered freely for their touches.

The four of them were a perfect match, and Durango knew he was home and they'd all be happy.

Forever.

THE END

HTTP://WWW.JANSPRINGER.COM

ABOUT THE AUTHOR

Jan Springer writes erotic romances at her secluded wilderness retreat nestled on four acres in cottage country, Minden Hills, Ontario Canada. Hobbies include kayaking, gardening, hiking, reading and writing. Jan writes full-time and is a member of the Romance Writers of America, Passionate Ink and the Authors Guild. She loves hearing from her readers.

Also by Jan Springer

Siren Classic: *Her Captive*
Ménage Amour: The Desperadoes 1: *The Pleasure Girl*
Ménage Amour: The Desperadoes 3: *Be My Dream Tonight*

Available at
BOOKSTRAND.COM

Siren Publishing, Inc.
www.SirenPublishing.com